Too Much

Love

To Hide

Maria and Zack
Summer Lake Seasons Book Two

By SJ McCoy

A Sweet n Steamy Romance

Published by Xenion, Inc

Published by Xenion, Inc.
First paperback edition 2019
www.sjmccoy.com

Cover Design by Dana Lamothe of Designs by Dana
Editor: Mitzi Pummer Carroll
Proofreaders: Aileen Blomberg, Marisa Nichols, Traci Atkinson.

ISBN 978-1-946220-51-6

Dedication

For Sam. Sometimes, life really is too short. Few x

Chapter One

"Thanks for bringing me back, guys." Clay smiled at Zack and Luke. "I know it was a late flight, but I figured we'd all rather get back here than stay in Nashville till tomorrow."

Luke grinned at him. "You know how I feel about it."

Clay nodded and grasped Zack's shoulder. "What about you, son?"

Zack smiled. "I'm happy to fly you wherever you want to go, whenever you want to go."

"And I appreciate it," said Clay. "I'd like to think this worked out well for you, too, though."

"I'm always happy to be back at Summer Lake. You know that."

Clay nodded and gave him an inquiring look. "I hope so. Are you still friendly with …" He shot a glance at Luke and changed his mind mid-sentence, "… with that friend of yours?"

"Yeah. I'm sure we'll catch up while I'm here."

"Okay. Well, we're all free and clear until a week from Monday. So, go have fun. I'll only call you for a flight if something urgent comes up and I don't think that's very likely." He smiled at Luke. "Go on, get out of here. I'm sure Angel's going to be thrilled you're home early."

Zack and Luke watched Clay climb into the SUV that his security guy, Adam, had pulled around in front of the building, then they walked across the parking lot to Zack's truck.

Once they were in and Zack had started the engine, Luke gave him a puzzled look. "What friend was Clay talking about?"

Zack met his gaze. He wanted to shrug it off. He'd managed to avoid the subject almost completely for a long time.

Luke raised an eyebrow. "Just one more thing you don't want to tell me about?"

"There's nothing to tell." He felt bad. He and Luke had been good friends for a few years now—ever since he'd first come to Summer Lake. They were close, but Zack still hadn't told him anything about his background. He was hoping the time was approaching that he'd be able to tell him everything. He blew out a sigh. The friend that Clay had been talking about had nothing to do with his past. There was no harm in telling Luke. "Okay, okay. I don't keep you in the dark because I don't trust you. It's just that there are some things about me you're better off not knowing."

"I know you have some super-secret past. Rumors have it that you're ex-mafia, ex-CIA, and a whole bunch of other things. I don't buy any of it. And you've promised me enough times that you'll tell me when the time is right. I'm good with that. I was just curious about this friend. I thought I was your friend." He gave Zack a mock hurt look. "I thought I knew all your friends—here at the lake, at least."

Zack laughed. "You do. This friend has nothing to do with my past; there's nothing secret about her."

"Maria?"

Zack nodded. "Yup. One time, I think it was the first time Clay came out here, he knew that by giving you a job in Nashville he was taking you away from Angel. He wondered if I had a girl here, too. He didn't believe that there was no one at all, and I told him that there was someone I liked, but that we're just friends."

"Why, though?"

"Because that's all we are."

"I know that, but why? Why aren't the two of you more than friends? You met her not long after I met Angel. We all know why it took Angel and me so long to get together. But I never figured out why you and Maria didn't. In the beginning, I thought the two of you were a sure thing, but then nothing came of it and—like everything else—you refused to talk about it."

Zack shrugged. "Because there's nothing to say." He put the truck in reverse and backed out. "We don't need to sit around here talking all night. Angel's going to be surprised enough that you're home tonight. We should get you there before she goes to bed, or you might scare her."

"So, you're just going to shut me down and refuse to tell me about Maria again?" Luke asked as they pulled away from the airport.

"Like I said, there's nothing to tell. Sure, I find her attractive—very attractive. I think she's an awesome person."

"So, why have you never asked her out?"

"Because ..." Zack didn't know how to explain anything without explaining everything, which was why he'd never tried. "You know that mysterious past of mine?"

Luke nodded.

"It makes it so that I'm better off not getting close to anyone."

"For your sake or theirs?"

"Both." He hadn't allowed himself to get close to anyone for years. He'd come to Summer Lake with the intention of keeping things that way. He hadn't intended to become such good friends with Luke, but it'd been unavoidable—Luke was such a good guy. But Luke was different. It wasn't the same as getting involved with a woman—a woman he could care about. And within a few weeks, he'd known that Maria was a woman he could care about—very much.

They drove on in silence for a while until Luke looked over at him again. "I hope someday you can deal with your past and allow yourself to a have a future."

"Thanks, bro. Me, too. Anyway, are you going to call Angel and let her know you're almost home?"

Luke grinned. "Nah. I want to surprise her."

That made Zack smile. "I think with any other woman, I'd be worried about what you might find—coming home early on a Friday night and surprising her. But with Angel, I know damned well that the worst you might discover is that she's still at work. You two are good together. Made for each other."

Luke nodded happily. "We are. I hope one day you find what we have. Maybe you and—"

Zack held up a hand to stop him before he said Maria's name. He'd heard it too many times tonight, and every time it made him wish for what he knew he couldn't have.

"What do you say, ladies? One more glass?" Angel stood in the doorway from the kitchen waving a bottle of wine.

Maria laughed. "Yeah, why not?" She looked at Roxy. "We know how to live it up on a Friday night, right girlfriend?"

Roxy laughed with her. "Sure, we do. I mean, who needs to go over to the resort and listen to the band? We can have a good time right here at Angel's—with face masks and wine. I'll have one more glass, but then I'll have to stop. I hate to be a party pooper, but I'm going to have to call a cab soon."

Angel came into the living room and refilled both their glasses. "You're no party pooper, Roxy. I'm not sure I'll even make it through another glass before I fall asleep. You're both welcome to stay over, though. Tonight has been so much fun. Why don't we do this more?"

Roxy laughed. "Because you're usually either working or with Luke. And that's not a complaint—at least, the Luke part isn't. I know I speak for us both ..." she nodded at Maria, "... when I say we are very happy for you. But you still need to take more time off from work when he's away. Tonight's been awesome. And thanks, it's tempting to stay, but I'd rather get back to my own bed, then I can sleep in tomorrow, and after all this wine, I'm going to need to."

She nodded again at Maria who had to laugh. "It has been a lot of fun, and I'm up for doing it again whenever. Though maybe not the face masks next time?"

"And why's that?" asked Roxy.

Maria laughed again. "Because you look like some kind of drunken clown—big silly grin on your face, nodding away to yourself like that." She reached up and patted her own cheek. "We should wash them off. They've been on a long time now."

"Finish your wine first," said Angel. "Do you want to stay?"

"I will if you want me to." Maria would rather go home, but the way Angel kept asking made her wonder if she wanted some company.

"No. It's fine. I'm hoping Luke will be home early in the morning, so I'd be rushing you out of here anyway." Angel chuckled. "Maybe it's because I feel guilty about that, that I keep offering for you to stay."

"In that case, no way. I don't have to go into work tomorrow, so I want to sleep late and have a lazy morning."

"Drink wine. Call taxi. Remove face goop," said Roxy.

Maria had to laugh. "I want to think that it's because you've had a little too much wine, but you always make me laugh."

Roxy gave her a happy smile. "That's okay. You're making me laugh, too, right now. You're always so pretty and put together, but you look a lot like a clown yourself with the face goop on."

Angel sat down on the sofa beside her. "She's right. We all do. But who cares? No one's going to see us. And I love this. I never thought I'd have girlfriends I could hang out with like this and do girly stuff. I love you guys."

Roxy leaned in, and they all hugged. Maria squeezed them tight. She loved them both. She might have only known them for a couple of years, but they were the best friends she'd ever had. Unlike Angel, she'd always had lots of friends, but until she'd come to Summer Lake, she hadn't had close friends—not like Angel and Roxy. She knew that the two of them would always be there for her, and she would do anything for them.

Angel sat up looking a little embarrassed. It wasn't like her to get so emotional. "Sorry, I might be a little tipsy, but it's not just the wine talking. I really do love you."

"And we love you, too," said Maria.

Roxy hiccupped and grinned at them. "We do. It's true."

Maria took her glass away from her. "I think you've had enough. Why don't you go and wash your face and I'll call us a cab."

Roxy gave them a sheepish look. "Sorry, girls. I'm not that bad."

"I know, but any more and you will be. It's getting late anyway."

"Okay." Roxy made her way into the little powder room in the hallway.

Angel smiled at Maria. "What are you going to do with your weekend?"

"As little as possible. I love having both days off, and it happens so rarely. I might take my camera out for a hike, but other than that, I'm just going to chill at home."

"Luke talked about going to the Boathouse tomorrow for dinner. Do you want to come?"

Maria shrugged. "Not if it's just the two of you, but let me know if there's a bunch of people going? I haven't heard the band play in ages."

"I'll call you, but I think he meant for us to meet up with everyone—not just us."

"Okay, if that's the case, I'm in. Call me." She dug her cell phone out of her purse. "I'm going to call us a cab. If Miss Tipsy hurries up in there, I should have time to wash my face before it gets here."

Angel laughed. "Are you okay in there, Roxy?" she called.

"Doing fine. Don't worry about me. I'll be back."

The dispatcher told Maria he could have a car outside in ten minutes. "Come on, Roxy. Time's up. I need to wash my face before we leave."

Roxy opened the door and stood there grinning at them. "All done." She swept her arm toward the powder room as she came out. "In you go, madam."

Maria stepped inside and closed the door behind her. No sooner had she done that than she heard the doorbell ring. Damn! That was quick. There must have a been a cab just around the corner.

Her heart started to pound when she heard the front door open and Angel squeal. "Oh, my God!"

She heard a man make a weird sound and then footsteps came into the hallway—footsteps that weren't Angel and Roxy.

Time seemed to stand still while her heart and mind raced. Her friends were in danger! She looked around for something—anything—she could use as a weapon. There was nothing—it was a powder room after all. She eyed the towel rail and pulled at it. She stepped backward and thudded against the wall as it came away in her hand; she hadn't expected it to. She'd lost the advantage of surprise by making that noise. The powder room door flew open, and she raised the rail and screamed, ready to defend herself and her friends against the intruder.

Her scream turned to a gasp when she saw the man standing there. He gasped, too, and took a step back at the sight of her.

"Maria? Are you okay?" Angel appeared beside Zack.

Maria stared at them both wishing the floor would open and swallow her up. Was she okay? Hell, no! She almost wished it *was* an attacker who'd flung the door open. Even that would be better than having gorgeous, sexy Zack standing there with that horrified look on his face! She still had a face mask on—white of course—so her eyes and mouth must have looked like something out of a horror movie when she screamed at him. And she was still … she slowly lowered the towel rail that she realized she was still holding up ready to strike.

Zack backed slowly away. Maria couldn't help it. She started to laugh. "I thought … when I heard the doorbell … and then you opened the door and screamed … I thought it was someone ... I dunno." She held the towel rail up apologetically. "I'll fix it for you."

Angel chuckled, and Luke and Roxy crowded around the doorway, too.

"Sorry, Maria," said Luke. "It's my fault. We got back tonight instead of in the morning. I wanted to surprise Angel."

"But I surprised him," said Angel with a smile. "I forgot I had my face mask on, and I thought it was your taxi. So, I opened the door..."

Luke laughed. "And scared the life out me!"

Maria shot a glance at Zack. If she'd still had any lingering hopes that something might happen between them one day, she'd dashed them tonight. "Not as much as I scared you, right, Zack?"

He smiled. He'd either recovered from his shock and horror or was hiding it well. "I'm not going to lie, but to be fair, you looked like you were about to batter me to death with—what is that?"

She looked down. "Towel rail ... or at least it used to be."

He held her gaze for a moment in that way he had. When she first knew him, she used to think he meant something by it—that he felt something between them the same way she did. But she knew better now. "You're quite something, Maria."

She wished that he might mean that in the way she wanted to take it, but she had to stop thinking about him that way. He was a friend, that was all. He was being a good sport about her almost beating him with a towel rail while screaming—and looking—like a banshee.

She gave him a rueful smile. "Aren't I just?"

Chapter Two

They all turned at the sound of the doorbell ringing. "That'll be my ride," said Roxy with a grin.

Zack liked her, she was always up for a laugh and seemed to be two sheets to the wind tonight.

"Can you ask him to wait a few minutes?" asked Maria. She gave Zack a rueful smile. "I need to wash my face before I scare the life out of anyone else. I look like a walking horror movie."

Zack wanted to tell her she was beautiful, even with that white stuff caked all over her face. He was hardly going to say it in front of the others—and what the hell was he thinking anyway? He couldn't tell her even if they were alone. The temptation to do so would be stronger, but no matter how beautiful he thought she was, there was nothing he could do about it, so there was no point mentioning it.

"I doubt he'll wait." Roxy gave Zack an exaggerated wink. At least, if it was supposed to be subtle, it failed miserably. "And besides, I need to go." Roxy grinned around at the others. "Let me know if we're all getting together this weekend? But not before lunchtime tomorrow."

"What about me?" asked Maria. "I need to get home, too."

"But you still have to wash your face. The taxi isn't going to wait—because I won't let him. And you ..." She swung her head to look at Zack. "You aren't staying here, are you? You still need to drive home to that fancy house of yours, and you have to pass Maria's place on your way there. While my house is in the opposite direction." She nodded happily, her point made. "I'm leaving. You're taking Maria home. Ladies and gentlemen, goodnight." She opened the front door to see the cab driver walking back down the path.

Zack looked around at the others. "Do you think she's okay to go?"

Angel nodded. "She's fine. She had a glass of wine too many, maybe. But that's Keith who's driving the cab. He'll make sure she gets home okay. He won't leave till she's safely inside."

"Okay." Zack didn't know what to do with the opportunity Roxy had just presented him with—the chance to drive Maria home. And he couldn't even think about it till he knew Roxy was going to get home safe.

"I'll call her in a few minutes," said Maria. "Tell her she has to text me once she's home." She looked up at Zack. "Would you mind giving me a ride?"

"Not at all." He wondered why his voice always sounded weird when he got around her.

"Thanks." She waved the towel rail at him. "I'll just see if I can put this back and then wash my face." She went back into the powder room and closed the door.

Luke caught Zack's eye and raised an eyebrow, but Zack just shook his head. He knew what his friend was thinking. But just because fate—in the form of a tipsy Roxy—was offering him a little time alone with Maria, it didn't mean he could act any differently toward her than he had been doing. She was his friend. That was all she could be.

Maria scrubbed at her face, regretting ever having put the stupid face mask on. Zack must think she was an idiot—and a scary-looking idiot at that. But at least she hadn't scared him out of giving her a ride home. She'd have to thank Roxy tomorrow—bless her slightly-sozzled heart. When the last of the mask was gone, she dried her face with the towel and then inspected herself. She didn't look too bad. Of course, she had no makeup on, which wasn't ideal, but then bare-faced was still better than clown-faced. She smiled at herself. There was no point making a big deal out of any of it. Zack wasn't interested in her. She might try to read too much into things he said and did sometimes, but if he were interested in her, surely, he would have said something by now.

When they first met, she'd thought he liked her, and she was damned sure she liked him—he was gorgeous! But either she'd been too optimistic, which was a flaw of hers, or his interest had only been fleeting. What had seemed like it might be a promising beginning had never amounted to anything, and they'd settled instead into a comfortable friendship. At least, it was mostly comfortable, as long as she remembered not to let her imagination get carried away.

She took a deep breath before she opened the powder room door and stepped out with a smile. The others had moved into the kitchen. Luke was sitting at the table, and Angel was sitting on his lap. It was time to get out of here. She might have given Zack a nasty surprise tonight, but Luke had given Angel a lovely surprise by coming home early. The two of them were looking at each other as though they wanted to capitalize on their good fortune just as soon as they could.

She met Zack's gaze. "Ready when you are."

He winked at her. "Yeah, don't get up, you guys. We'll see ourselves out."

Angel smiled at Maria. "I'll call you tomorrow."

"Don't worry if not. You two have some catching up to do."

Luke smiled at her. "We do, but we're going out tomorrow night with everyone. You should come."

Angel gave her a wicked smile. "Especially since you have the whole weekend off for once."

She felt Zack's head turn toward her but continued looking at Angel. "Call me."

Luke looked at Zack. "You're coming out tomorrow night, right?"

"I am, but right now what I'm doing is leaving." He smiled at Maria, and she nodded.

"See you guys," she called as she made her way to the front door. When she reached it, she closed her eyes for a moment as his arm reached past her to open it. She could feel him close behind her. She could smell him. He smelled so good; he always did. He smelled like sandalwood—and man. She pulled herself together and went through the door and down the path to where his truck was waiting.

He opened the passenger door for her and grinned. She'd ridden in his truck before—usually when a whole bunch of them went somewhere together, but occasionally just the two of them. It was so damned big, she struggled to climb up.

"Do you want a boost?" he asked with a smile.

She shook her head and grabbed the handle inside the door to haul herself up. Once she was settled in the passenger seat, she smiled at him. "Thanks, but I'm good."

He gave her that weird look of his. "Yes, you are," he said before he closed the door and made his way around to the driver's side. Sometimes she wondered if she pissed him off.

He started the engine and looked over at her.

She smiled. "Thanks for this. I hope it's not putting you out."

He shook his head. "It's my pleasure."

She wanted to tell him that the pleasure was all hers. She loved any moments she got to spend alone with him. But he didn't need to know that.

"Should you call Roxy?" he asked as he pulled the truck out onto the street.

"Yeah." She took her phone out of her purse. He was right. She should check on her friend instead of hoping to spend the next few minutes catching up with him.

She dialed the number and listened to it ring.

"Maria! What's wrong?"

"I wanted to make sure you got home safe."

"Of course, I did. *I* wanted to make sure that *you* got to go home with Zack. It's about time the two of you got together. I just did my bit. You can thank me any time."

"Mm-hmm."

"Mm-hmm? Is that all I get? I set you up to spend some time alone with big sexy Zack in his big sexy truck, and all you can say is mm-hmm? Why?"

Maria wanted to laugh. "Think about it."

"Think about what ... oh ... you're still in the sexy truck with the sexy Zack?"

"Yes." Maria shot a glance over at him, wondering if he had any clue how this conversation was going. He didn't seem to. He kept his gaze fixed on the road ahead.

"So, why are you calling me? Go away."

Maria had to laugh. "Okay. Now I know you're home safe."

"Call me tomorrow? I need to hear all about it."

"I will. And you do me a favor and leave a glass of water and a couple of aspirin on your nightstand before you go to sleep? I have a feeling you're going to need them when you wake up."

Roxy groaned. "Oh. Good thinking. I will. You're right. Goodnight. Have fun."

"Thanks. Goodnight, Roxy."

She ended the call and put her phone back in her purse.

"I take it she's okay?"

"She is. She's home safe. I think she's going to have a bit of a hangover in the morning, though."

Zack smiled. "It's funny. I would never think of you girls hitting the booze hard."

"We didn't. Not really. It's just that none of us really drinks much so anything more than a couple of glasses of wine and we're tipsy."

He turned and met her gaze for a moment before looking back at the road and asking. "Are you? Tipsy?"

For some reason that made her tummy flip over and her heart rate pick up. Did he want her to be? No! Of course, he didn't. He was probably just trying to figure out the reason for her crazy behavior when he and Luke had arrived. "A little. I guess. It's no excuse though."

Deep furrows creased his brow. She'd noticed those before and figured he must do a lot of thinking to have etched them so deeply. "Excuse? For what?"

"For almost attacking you earlier."

He laughed. "I have to tell you, you scared the life out of me."

She rolled her eyes. "Sorry."

"Hey. No. No need to say sorry. I think it's kind of cool. Most girls would have curled up in the corner crying if they thought there were intruders in the house. Not you. You were coming out fighting. I admire that."

Warmth spread through her chest. He admired her?! She thought *that* was kind of cool. She shrugged. "It's just the way I am. I thought the girls were in trouble. I had to do what I could to help them—to protect them. I look out for my own."

He shot a glance at her. "I do, too." The words sounded like they were loaded with meaning when he said them, but she had no idea what that meaning might be.

Her heart sank when he turned into her street. How sad was that? He was only giving her a ride home as a friend. It wasn't like they'd been on a date or anything. It wasn't the end of an evening spent together—just a favor that he'd brought her home.

He pulled up in front of her house, and she looked over at him. "Thanks, Zack."

He nodded and cut the engine, making her heart start racing again.

"Anytime."

She nodded. She should say something, but she didn't know what. Maybe she had had too much wine. They'd hung out together before. He'd given her rides home from the Boathouse and the Lodge when everyone had been out together. She smiled. She needed to get this back on their usual footing—or at least remember that tonight was no different from usual. He was her friend, and it was only the wine that made tonight feel like it could be anything more than that.

"How long are you back for?"

"Until a week from Monday."

"Wow, that's a long stretch. What are you going to do with yourself?"

~ ~ ~

Zack held her gaze for a moment. "I don't know." He didn't know why, but everything felt different between them tonight. Maybe it was because Luke had asked about her on the drive back from the airport. Maybe it was seeing her brandishing a towel rail at him while looking like a demented clown. Something had changed. He'd always been attracted to her, but tonight, for the first time, he didn't know how long he'd be able to hide that from her.

He shrugged. Maybe he wouldn't have to keep hiding it for much longer anyway. He tightened his grip on the steering wheel. No. He couldn't afford to relax now—not when the end was almost in sight. He couldn't take any risks, but being her friend wasn't a risk. He could do that. "Angel said you have the weekend off. Do you want to hang out?"

She nodded slowly. Her eyes searched his face. Did she feel it too? Did she know that something had shifted between them tonight and did she feel—like he did—that there'd be no shifting it back?

"Do you want to have lunch tomorrow?" That was nothing risky; they'd done that before—many times.

She nodded again and then seemed to pull herself together. "That'd be great. Do you mind if I call you? I think I'll be sleeping late in the morning. I don't want to commit to anything too early."

"Sure." He didn't either.

"Okay … well …" She reached for the door handle. "Thanks again."

As she turned, he could see a smear of white still on her cheek. He leaned toward her. "Come here."

Her eyes widened, but she leaned toward him.

In that moment, he knew she felt it, too. He reached his hand up to her cheek and smoothed away the white powder from her face. "You still had …"

She nodded, her gaze locked with his, and instead of bringing his hand down, he slid his fingers into her hair.

Her tongue ran over her lips, and he had to watch. He'd waited a long time—way too long—to kiss those lips. He leaned closer in and … sat back up in a hurry when the sound of a car alarm cut through the quiet of the street.

Maria sat back, too, as if she'd been slapped. She looked shocked. "I'm sorry. I should go." She reached for the door handle again and this time didn't hesitate on the way out.

"Call me when you're ready in the morning?"

She turned back to look at him before she closed the door.

"You're still going to call me, right?" Zack's heart was pounding. He was afraid he'd blown it.

She nodded but didn't look convinced.

"If you don't call me, I'll call you," he told her. There was no way he was going to let a near-miss kiss spoil things between them.

"Okay." He hoped that was almost a smile she gave him before she closed the truck door.

He watched her walk up the path to her front door. If she went straight in without looking back, he'd know he'd blown it. He held his breath while he watched her dig her keys out of her purse. She unlocked the door and stepped inside. "Come on," he murmured under his breath.

She turned around and looked straight at him. A wave of relief swept over him. He gave her what he hoped was a reassuring smile. She was in. She was scared, but she was in.

He held up a hand, and she gave him a small wave before she closed the door.

He started the truck with a smile on his face, but it soon faded as he pulled away and remembered that, even if she wanted to be in with him, he couldn't put her at risk like that.

Chapter Three

When Carter turned into the driveway, Summer smiled at the sight of the house. She really did love the place. She'd only stayed here for a short time, but it had felt like a sanctuary. A safe place to hide and to rest. It was so beautiful, sitting as it did on the bank of the Yellowstone, with glorious views of the mountains all around.

Carter brought the truck to a stop outside the front door then looked over at her. "What time did you tell Cassidy we'd be over for dinner?" he asked.

"Seven."

He nodded and looked at the clock on the dash. "In that case, I'll bring your bags in for you and leave you to get settled. I need to head home to shower and change."

She hadn't been expecting that. He'd agreed that they could talk when he got her here. "But…" she croaked.

He shook his head with a finality she recognized. "But nothing. You need to rest your voice for more than just an hour. I need to get cleaned up and changed. There's nothing to argue about."

She nodded. She knew he was right. But she wasn't giving up, either. She climbed out of the truck and followed him up the steps. Once she'd unlocked the front door, he brought her bags inside.

"Where do you want them?"

She pointed down the hallway to her bedroom. Carter stopped in the doorway, looking uncomfortable.

Summer couldn't help smiling. He'd been over here a few times during her last visit, but she knew he was uncomfortable *invading her private space* as he'd put it. He'd made a big effort to stay out on the deck whenever he came, only venturing in as far as the living room when she insisted. She gestured toward the bed, knowing that would make him more uncomfortable still. As he placed her bags on it, she sat down and smiled up at him. "Thank you."

He nodded and backed away. He didn't stop until he reached the door. When he did he blocked the light.

She wished he'd come back, come sit beside her, talk to her, be honest with her about how he felt, let her be honest about how she felt. "Do you have to go right now?" she asked.

He'd taken his hat off and was twisting it in his hands as he stood there. He held her gaze for a long moment before he nodded. "I do. Get some rest. I'll come pick you up around six thirty." He turned on his heel and left.

She was tempted to run after him, but she knew there was no point. He'd be back in a couple of hours, and hopefully, by then she'd be able to talk for a little while—rather than croak or whisper, which seemed to be all she was capable of right now. She heard the front door close and a few moments later his truck pulled away. She lay back on the bed and stared up at the ceiling. What was she going to do? What could she do? She had no idea. She knew she wanted to do something. Carter was her ideal man—both physically and in personality. She'd told

Cassidy that it seemed as though someone upstairs had listened to everything she wanted in a man and had put Carter together, especially for her. He was kind, he was sweet, he was caring. He knew who he was, he loved his life, and he loved his work. She sighed. And his life and his work were right here in Paradise Valley. How could they get involved with each other when she would probably be leaving in three months' time— and he would never leave! At the same time, wouldn't it be crazy not to explore what they both obviously felt for each other? How would they be able to avoid it? Unless they avoided each other, which seemed to be Carter's solution. She shook her head. She wasn't going to let him get away with that. She wanted to spend time with him, even if it was only as friends.

She got up from the bed and went through to the bathroom. She couldn't kid herself that just friends would be enough. She started the water running. She wanted to sit in the tub and stare out the window at the mountain while she mulled it all through.

~ ~ ~

When Carter got home, he let himself in through the back door. He kicked his boots off and hung his hat in the mudroom. He picked up the coffee mug he'd left on the kitchen table this morning and rinsed it out. What a difference a day made! This morning, he'd known that Summer was coming back and he was determined to stick to his plan to avoid her. Now here he was, not twelve hours later, and he'd already picked her up from the airport, told her she'd made him feel like the happiest guy on earth, and if that wasn't enough, he was going back to see her later and taking her to dinner with his brother and Cassidy!

He tidied the kitchen. He loved this house. He'd built it the third year the nursery did well. The nursery covered five acres, and when the five next door had come up for sale, he'd bought the lot and built his home next to his business. It wasn't anything grand, but it was nice. It was his. He went out back and stopped to pet a cat who came curling around his legs. "Hey, Buster," he said as he scratched behind his ears. "How you doing? Are you keeping the mice down for me?"

Buster purred loudly in reply and rubbed his head against Carter's leg.

Carter smiled. "Yeah, right. I'll fill up you guys' food." He left food out for a whole bunch of cats who hung around out here. He claimed that they kept the mice down, but in reality he was just a soft ass and didn't like to admit it. He was so soft, in fact, that he'd turned one of sheds into a home for the cats. Buster had been the first stray to show up around here a couple of years ago. Carter had invited him to come stay in the house, but he didn't like to be cooped up. Carter had taken to leaving food and warm blankets out in the shed—the shed that had a broken board where a cat could squeeze in if they really wanted to. Buster had made the place his home, and then he started inviting his friends over. Nowadays there were at least a half dozen of them who hung out on any given night.

Once he'd filled up their food and made sure they had fresh water, he let himself back into the house. It was time to take a shower and figure out what he was going to wear tonight. He chuckled to himself—what was he, a girl? But it was important to him. He wanted to look good. He opened his closet and stared in there. It shouldn't be important, but it was. He'd already proved to himself that he wasn't going to be able to stay away from Summer. He'd already been more honest than he should have with her about how he felt. And she hadn't been horrified. He knew she liked him. He was starting to wonder whether he should just keep being honest—with himself as well as with her. He'd spent ten years of his life avoiding women, trying to save himself from more pain. Maybe Summer was the one who would help him get past that? He knew that life didn't happen without pain, but if you were going to take the risk, the potential reward had to be worthwhile. He couldn't think of any greater potential reward than Summer. If he wasn't prepared to take a risk on her, then he may as well hang up his boots right now.

He closed the closet door again. He'd figure it out after his shower. For now he headed for the bathroom and set the water running. He needed to get cleaned up and hopefully wash some of his fear and confusion away.

He pulled up back at her house at six thirty on the dot. She must have been watching for him; the front door opened as he climbed out of his truck. He smiled. She was so damned beautiful! She was small and fragile looking, but there was a strength about her, too. A strength he admired. She was dressed casual tonight in black jeans and a long white sweater. Her long blonde hair fell loose around her shoulders. She took his breath away. She waved and he started toward her, realizing that he'd been standing there staring like an idiot.

"How are you feeling?" he asked when he reached the door.

She nodded. "Better." She smiled up at him. "And you'll be relieved to hear that I think we should get going."

He raised an eyebrow. He wasn't relieved; if anything, he was a little disappointed. He'd been looking forward to a few minutes alone with her, before they went to Cassidy's place.

She laughed. "I'm not letting you off the hook. I still want us to talk, but I have to be realistic about how long my voice will last. I want to get to Cassidy's, have dinner, and then get you back here."

He shook his head with a smile. "We won't be able to get away from their place early, and knowing you and Cassidy, your voice will be all used up in the first half hour anyway. I think I'm safe for tonight."

She surprised the hell out of him when she stepped toward him, put her hands on his shoulders and stood on tiptoe to kiss his cheek. "Don't you believe it, Carter. You'll never be safe from me!"

He sucked in a deep breath as she stood back with a smile. It took everything he had not to close his arms around her and pull her against him. Maybe he needed to go back to his plan of avoiding her, because letting her get as close as she just had would only end up leading them to one place. The way the blood was rushing through his veins, pounding in his temples, he wanted to forget about their evening out and take her to that one place right now!

She misread his reaction and looked concerned. "Was that too much?"

He shook his head.

"What then?"

"It wasn't enough." Damn! He shouldn't have said it. But he'd had no choice. It was the truth.

Her eyes widened and two little spots of pink appeared on her cheeks. Then a smile slowly spread across her face. "I agree."

Oh, shit! What was he supposed to do with that? What he supposed to say even? "Come on, we'd better get going." He turned around and headed back to the truck. It was the only safe thing to do.

~ ~ ~

When they arrived at Cassidy's, Shane flung the door open and greeted them with a grin. "Welcome back, Summer! Come on in. The little lady is in the kitchen; I've got her chained to the stove."

Summer laughed and reached up to hug him as he held his arms out to her. She liked Shane. He was the perfect guy for Cassidy. "It's good to see you again, Shane."

"Come on through," called Cassidy. "And if you can manage to lock that asshole out on the porch when you come in, that'd be great."

Shane grinned at Summer and Carter. "She loves me really."

Carter laughed. "I don't know how she puts up with you."

Shane feigned a hurt look and put an arm around Summer's shoulders as he walked her through to the kitchen. "I'm glad you're back. You're the only one who's ever nice to me. These guys are mean!"

Summer smiled at Cassidy who was, indeed, at the stove. She smiled back as she waved a wooden spoon at Shane with a grin. "She does, but if you don't get out of this kitchen and out of my way…"

Shane let go of Summer and held up both hands. "Consider me gone!" He looked at Carter. "Come on, bro. The kitchen's no place for guys to be hanging out anyways. Come on out on the deck with me. We can leave the little women to it."

Summer laughed as the wooden spoon flew through the air, just missing Shane's ear. "Get out while you still can!"

"Yes, dear. Love you, dear," called Shane as the door closed behind them.

"I see you're settling in to nearly-wedded bliss, then," Summer said when the guys had gone.

Cassidy laughed. "We are. It's wonderful. I love that asshole to pieces!"

"I can tell. Oh, and let me see the ring! Typical that you went and got engaged as soon as I left."

Cassidy wiped her hands and came around the island to show Summer her engagement ring.

"Oh, Cass! It's beautiful. Congratulations!"

The smile on Cassidy's face said it all. She was happier than Summer had ever seen her. It was obvious that she'd found her match in Shane. She gave Summer a hug. "Thank you! And what about you? How have you been?" She shot a look toward the door. "How's Carter?"

Summer couldn't help smiling. "Carter is wonderful! You know I adore him."

Cassidy nodded. "So, my flat tire came at a good time?"

Summer had wondered about the timing. "Did you really have one?"

Cassidy shrugged. "Might have. Might not. All that matters is that you got a ride home."

"Thank you."

"I need more than that! How did it go? What's he said? What's going to happen with you two?"

"If only I knew what's going to happen. I have no idea. It was so wonderful to see him at the airport. But he told me he was planning to avoid me while I'm here. I understand why—and it might be the wisest thing to do. But, Cass, I don't want him to. I want to spend time with him. I want him to be my friend."

Cassidy snorted. "You were doing well, but don't start lying to me. You do *not* want him to be your friend. You want a whole lot more than that. And so does he. I can tell."

Summer nodded. "You're right. As always. But what do we do about it? Neither of us do casual, and casual is all it could be. His life is here. My life is in Nashville."

Cassidy gave her a stern look. "And have you given any thought to your life in Nashville? To your career? Last time we talked about it, you weren't even sure you wanted to keep singing—even if you could."

Summer heaved a big sigh. "Honestly. I haven't wanted to think about it. I feel as though I'd be jinxing myself."

Cassidy raised an eyebrow.

She shrugged. "I daren't let my mind go near the thought of stopping singing, because…well, I know it sounds silly, but…it feels as though I'm being ungrateful. Singing has been the best thing that's happened to me. If I think about giving it up, it might be taken away from me."

"Taken away from you?"

"I might not get my voice back. I might not be *able* to sing again. Like I said, I know it's silly. In fact it's probably just an excuse not to make any decisions until I have to."

Cassidy nodded. "That sounds more like it."

"Yeah, well I'm not Miss Head-on Full-on like you are. I don't want to face it until I have to."

"So what's your plan? Take three months here, see what the doctors say and then decide?"

"Yeah, that's about it."

"And what happens to Autumn in the meantime? And Carter, for that matter?"

Summer shrugged. That was the problem. She didn't want to make any decisions about her career until she had to, but there were other decisions that she *did* want to make. Decisions that would depend on what happened with her career. "I don't know, Cass! I don't want to hurt either of them. I don't want to screw either of them over, but how can I know anything, until I know whether I can sing again?" She could hear the croak in her voice as she finished—so much for not overdoing it!

Cassidy put a hand on her shoulder. "You need to decide what you want, not wait to see what's possible."

Summer nodded. She could only expect that from Cassidy, that's what she herself would do—take life by the horns and wrestle with it till it submitted to her will. Summer was more used to going along with whatever life dictated and making the most of it. It wasn't that she wasn't strong. It was just that life had always dealt her a pretty decent hand and she made the most of the opportunities presented to her. She'd never been in this kind of situation before—where she needed to figure out what she wanted and go after it, for the sake of the people she cared about as much as her own.

"Do you know what you want?"

She shrugged. She thought she did, but everything she wanted conflicted with something else she wanted! Deep down, she already knew she wanted to quit her career. But she didn't want to leave Autumn in the lurch—her sister's career was dependent upon her own. She didn't want to let Clay down either. He'd been so good to her and he had such faith in her. Much as she didn't want to let them down, she *did* want to see what might happen between her and Carter. And the only way to do that would be to decide that she was going to stay right here. How could she get involved with him if she knew she might have to break things off and go back to Nashville? He'd loved and lost before and it had broken his heart. She had no intention of being the woman who put him through that a second time.

Cassidy patted her shoulder. "Take a little time. You'll work it out. I'll help if you want me. Just…" She looked toward the door at the sound of the guys laughing out on the deck. "Don't take too long. I'd hate to see Carter get hurt."

Summer nodded sadly. So would she.

"I'd hate to see *you* get hurt, too. And I think the longer you put off making your decision, the more likely that is. Be brave. Be honest with Carter; be honest with Autumn. You'll work it out. But for now, put a smile back on your face and give me a hand."

"Okay." Summer was happy to make herself useful rather than carry on with this conversation which was making her so uncomfortable. Cassidy had made her realize that she had to make some decisions sooner rather than later. She was going to have to *direct* the flow of her life instead of just waiting around to go with it.

Chapter Four

Maria rolled over and looked at the clock on her nightstand. She groaned. Eight o'clock. That wasn't much of a lie in. She closed her eyes again and burrowed deeper under the covers, but it was no use. Her mind had already started racing—racing its way back to last night, to Zack's truck, to Zack.

She pulled the pillow over her head and screwed her eyes tightly shut. Even then, all she could see was his face—the horrified look on it when he'd opened the powder room door and seen her brandishing a towel rail, the indecipherable look he'd given her when he told her she was quite something. She groaned. In her imagination, the way he'd looked at her when he'd told her to *come here* when he'd reached over and touched her cheek had looked a lot like a guy who wanted her. She wasn't a stranger to that look. But it could only be her imagination. She'd gone and made a fool of herself, leaning in as if he were going to kiss her. Thank goodness for that car alarm.

She rolled over and sat up, propping the pillows against the headboard and leaning back on them. Still, even as she'd tried to flee the truck to save them both from her embarrassment, he'd said he wanted her to call him today—still wanted to have lunch with her. He was such a stand-up guy, he probably only said it to let her know everything was okay between them. That she hadn't ruined their friendship by being such an idiot.

She brought her knees up to her chest and hugged them. She kind of knew that wasn't the real reason he'd said he'd call her if she didn't call him. He liked her. Sitting here in the cold, clear light of morning, she knew it instinctively. She could make up as many excuses as she liked, but deep down she knew. He had wanted to kiss her. When he brushed the last of that damned face mask off her cheek, he'd sunk his fingers into her hair. She hadn't leaned toward him only because she was a fool—he'd been leaning toward her too. His gaze had dropped to her lips. If that car alarm hadn't gone off ...

A wave of heat rushed through her and settled between her legs. What might have happened? Would they have kissed? Made out right there in his truck? Would she have invited him in?

She shook her head. No. She wouldn't. Even if her instincts were right, she wouldn't be rushing into bed with him, would she? The heat pooled between her legs and her breasts tingled, suddenly sensitive to the cotton of her T-shirt brushing her nipples. No. If anything was going to happen, it didn't have to happen in a hurry. She flung back the covers and got out of bed. But as she looked herself in the eye in the mirror while she brushed her teeth, she couldn't help smiling. The naughty little voice in the back of her head was reminding her that there was nothing hurried about it. She'd known Zack for a long time now. And she'd known on the first day she met him that if he ever wanted to take her to bed—she wouldn't say no.

After she'd showered and eaten breakfast, she went back upstairs and made her bed. She'd told Zack that she wanted to sleep in. So? Since she hadn't managed to stay asleep, why shouldn't she call him now? At least that way they could make a plan for later and she'd know how long she had to spend in her closet deciding what on earth she should wear.

She picked her phone up and then set it down again. No. It was only nine-thirty. She could decide what she was going to wear first, then call him.

She went into her closet and stood there looking around. She loved clothes. She had a lot of nice clothes. It was a Saturday; they were going for lunch. What did it matter what she wore? It mattered a lot, according to her racing heart. She pulled down a vee neck sweater. It was purple, pretty, but still casual. She pulled it on and went to look in the mirror. It hugged her figure and was cut low enough to show a little cleavage—but not too much. She cocked her head to one side. It wasn't too much, was it? She blew out a sigh. Maybe it was. She pulled the sweater off and reached for a pink and white plaid shirt. That was fun, maybe a little flirty, but not too … She pulled that off, too. This was crazy. She'd had lunch with Zack dozens of times. She always made a little extra effort—she wouldn't deny that—but she'd never gotten this stupid before. Half an hour later, her usually neat closet looked like it had been hit by a tornado, and she still had no idea what she was going to wear. She ran back out into the bedroom at the sound of her phone ringing on the bed where she'd left it.

Her heart rate kicked into high gear when she saw Zack's name on the display. Her hands shook as she swiped to answer. "Hey."

"Hey." She loved the sound of his voice. It was all deep and manly. She'd always imagined it held the trace of an accent, but she'd never dared ask him about it. You didn't ask Zack personal questions like that.

"How are you?" she asked, then made a face to herself. That was a dumb question. She'd only spoken to fill the silence.

"I'm good. I hope it's not too early?"

"No. I've been up for a while."

"You didn't get to sleep in then?"

"No."

"It gets me that way sometimes, too."

Her heart leaped into her mouth. What did he mean? She hadn't slept well because her mind had been racing with thoughts about him—before she got to sleep and from the moment she came near the surface. Was he saying that sometimes he couldn't sleep because he was thinking about her? "What?" She hated that her voice came out as a squeak.

"The booze. Your body can't process it, and instead of getting a good rest, you end up not sleeping so well."

"Oh, yes." Of course, that was what he meant. "That must have been it."

"Since you're up, do you want to get together now?"

Excitement swept away her disappointment. "We can. What are you thinking?"

"That we could hang out for the day. Not just lunch. I'll come pick you up."

"Err …" She peered into the disarray in her closet.

"Whenever you're ready. You tell me what time."

She nodded to herself. The state of her closet didn't matter, and what she wore didn't really matter either. "Give me half an hour?"

"Sure. Want me to bring anything?"

"Just yourself."

"Okay. See you in a bit."

"Bye."

She hung up and hurried back into her closet. She pulled on her favorite jeans; they were comfortable—that was the most important consideration, not the fact that she knew they made her booty look great. She looked around wildly at the tops scattered all over the floor. This wasn't like her. She spotted the vee neck sweater she'd tried on first and put it on. If it showed off too much cleavage, it would only help her confirm whether her instincts were right.

~ ~ ~

Zack pulled up outside her house in the same spot he'd parked in last night. He'd spent the small hours wondering if he might have gone inside with her if that car alarm hadn't sounded. It would have been a mistake if he had—but a mistake he knew he wouldn't have regretted.

He grabbed a bag off the passenger seat and climbed out of the truck. When he'd spoken to her earlier, and she'd told him she hadn't been able to sleep in, it had made him wonder if she'd been tossing and turning thinking about last night, too. He had a feeling that maybe she had. He didn't know what his plan was for today. He wanted to let her know that he liked her, but he couldn't tell her why he couldn't act on it. At the same time, he wanted to act on it to show her in no uncertain terms just how much he liked her. He couldn't though, at least not for … who knew how long? She wasn't a girl he could just fool around with for a while. She was someone he wanted to get close to, and he couldn't get close to anyone.

He clutched the bag tighter as he walked up the path. He hoped she'd appreciate the gesture. He'd gone for a drive this morning—anything rather than sit in the house driving himself nuts with thoughts of what he could and couldn't do and say today. He'd ended up at the bakery in town where he'd bought her a box of her favorite chocolate croissants. A whole gang of them had gone for a picnic hike up above Four Mile Creek a couple of months ago, and she'd brought a box of the croissants. Watching her eat one had been an exquisite kind of torture. It'd made him even more desperate to know what she'd be like in bed. She'd made these appreciative little noises, savored every mouthful and even licked her fingers when she was done. His cock stirred at the memory. *Down boy.* He'd brought her some this morning because he knew she enjoyed them—not because he was hoping for a repeat performance.

He raised his hand to knock on the door, and it opened. He clenched his jaw in an attempt to stop a low whistle from escaping his lips. She always looked good to him, no matter what she wore, but this morning? Damn! He'd guess that she hadn't gone to any kind of special effort—she was one of those girls who was always well-groomed, well put together. She probably had no idea of the effect her outfit would have on him, but … damn … was the only word that came to mind.

Her heavy breasts looked as though they were trying to climb out of her sweater to greet him, and she was wearing a pair of jeans that had to be his favorites on her. They had a small tear just below her right knee—he neither knew nor cared if it was there by design or accident. All he knew was that that little tear had trained him over the last few months to expect to see her gorgeous, ample ass displayed perfectly for him when she turned around. He'd never gone so far as to start dropping things on the floor for her to pick up when she wore those jeans—but he'd been tempted.

"Hi, come on in."

She smiled and sounded breezy enough, but she didn't meet his gaze. He knew his assessment last night had been right. She was in. She was interested in him, open to seeing what might happen between them. How was he supposed to remember that nothing could while she looked like that?

He held up the bag. "I brought you some goodies."

"Ooh. Thank you. What did you get?"

He smiled. "Your favorites."

"Chocolate croissants?" Her smile lit up her face. She was adorable, eager as a small child, though there was nothing childlike about her figure.

"Yup."

"Come on through." She led him straight to the kitchen. "You do realize that you just delayed lunch a while?" she asked him with a smile. "I have no self-control when it comes to those things. I have to have them—and I have to have them now. Do you want a drink to go with them?"

Zack nodded. He couldn't help wishing that he could have the same effect on her. How would it be if she had no self-control when it came to him? If she had to have him and she had to have him now? He bit the inside of his lip. He couldn't let himself imagine how that might be, or he might end up being the one losing his self-control.

He took a seat at the table and watched as she poured them each a mug of coffee. Well, she could have been pouring orange juice or poison for all the attention he paid. He wasn't watching her hands but watching her ass. He had to shift in his seat as the interest stirred in his pants. Her ass was big and round and moved in the most inviting ways as she reached two mugs down from a cupboard and poured the coffee into them. He had to stifle a groan when she opened the fridge and bent down to get the milk out of the bottom shelf of the door.

She gave him a puzzled look when she straightened up, and he brought his hand up to his mouth and pretended to yawn. "Sorry. I didn't get enough sleep last night."

She nodded. "I know how you feel."

She brought the coffees to the table and sat down opposite him with a smile. "I'm so terrible. I can't wait to get some."

Zack swallowed hard. He would love to get some, too. Unfortunately, she was talking about chocolate croissants while he was thinking about her and her voluptuous body. He shifted in his seat again. He'd been attracted to her since he first met her. If he'd only been attracted to her body, then he would have done something about it by now, but it was more than that. She was fun, sweet, always upbeat, and positive. She lifted his spirits without even knowing it. He was attracted to her as a person, not just as a hot body. Which was a shame, really. His situation meant that he couldn't allow himself to get close to people. He wanted to get close to Maria in every sense. If he'd only wanted to get some, he would have made his move by now.

She gave a little groan of appreciation as she bit into a croissant. "Oh my God. That's so good."

He needed to focus. He couldn't allow his mind to do what it was doing—couldn't allow himself to imagine that her words and the little sounds she was making were about anything other than the croissant.

She set it down on the plate and raised an eyebrow at him. "Are you going to have one?"

He nodded and picked one up, taking a big bite in an attempt to divert his attention away from the crumb of chocolate in the corner of her mouth. What he wouldn't give to lick that crumb away.

She noticed it too and ran her finger over it, swiping the crumb into her mouth before sucking on the tip of her finger.

Zack took another big bite and closed his eyes while he chewed. He needed to stop it. Needed to get back on a regular footing. He wouldn't have been able to survive around her for this long if he hadn't managed to keep his imagination—and his desire in check. Things had shifted last night—gotten away from him—but he needed to put a lid on it or ... his next thought sobered him up in a hurry—or he wouldn't be able to hang out with her anymore. Watching her indulge her passion for chocolate croissants might be torture and make him stiff with desire to indulge in passion with her, but it was infinitely preferable to avoiding her completely, and that was what he'd have to do if he couldn't keep himself in check.

"Angel said you have the weekend off?" he asked, hoping to get things back on a normal footing.

She nodded. "Laura's in town, but Smoke's working away, so she gave me the day off. She knows I enjoy a Saturday to myself sometimes.

"And you don't mind that you're not getting it to yourself? I'm not spoiling any plans, am I?"

She shook her head rapidly. "I didn't have any. Well, I wanted to sleep in this morning, and that didn't work out. I had planned to maybe go for a hike over at Four Mile this afternoon, but it's supposed to rain so that wouldn't have worked out anyway." She met his gaze. "Sometimes you think you know what's going to happen, but then everything changes and morphs into something unexpected—and much better."

His heart raced. It felt like she was talking about him, about them. Was she telling him that she'd thought they were just friends and now—after last night—she knew things were changing between them, and she was happy about it?

He bit the inside of his lip. No. Of course, she wasn't. And even if she were, things couldn't change between them; not yet, at least. Still, the way she was looking at him made him wish they could. He smiled. "Well, since you didn't get to sleep in and you don't get to hike and there's not much that's going to be fun outside today, do you want to come and hang out at my place this afternoon? It strikes me as a good day to watch movies and veg out."

She smiled. "I'd love to. That's the kind of day I need, but I always feel too guilty to just laze around by myself."

He held her gaze for a moment. "You can always call me, you know. I'll always be up for spending the day lying around with you."

There was a flicker of something in her eyes. He couldn't tell if she was shocked or interested. He meant that how it had come out, but at the same time, he couldn't deny that one part of him was undeniably up at the thought of lying with her.

Chapter Five

The sound of Maria's phone ringing made Zack start. He sat up feeling guilty. They'd been lying on the sofa watching a movie. He'd managed to block out the voice of reason that was screaming inside his head that he shouldn't be allowing himself to do this. The phone brought him back to reality with a jolt.

She smiled at him. "I should see who it is." She leaned over the arm of the sofa and fished her phone out of her purse. Even now, he couldn't help admiring the way her rounded ass filled out his sweatpants so nicely. "It's Angel. I should take it."

Zack nodded. "I'll go fix us a drink."

He went into the kitchen and stood there for a moment, gripping the edge of the island with both hands, letting his head hang down. What was he playing at? Why had he allowed himself to weaken? He'd managed to keep his attraction to her under wraps for over a year. So, why had his self-control crumbled in less than twenty-four hours? Only last night, he'd told Luke that he couldn't allow himself to get close to her. This afternoon, here he was lying on the sofa with her—within a hair's breadth of taking her upstairs to his bed.

He poured them each a soda and listened to the sound of her voice. She had such a sweet voice. He shook his head. He wasn't trying to eavesdrop on her conversation. He should occupy himself with something else so that he didn't listen in. He checked his own phone. There was a text from Luke, asking if he was coming to the Boathouse tonight. He'd forgotten about that. Kenzie had asked at lunch if he was going to bring Maria. She'd said yes. Right now, he had no desire to go and hang out with everyone. He'd much prefer to stay right here to lie back down on the sofa with her, curl his arm around her and … His cock stood to attention at what his imagination conjured up could happen next. It couldn't happen though. He blew out a sigh. Talk about a rock and hard place. He didn't want to take her out because he didn't want it to become public knowledge that they were together— and they weren't—not really, not yet. At the same time, he couldn't afford to stay in with her because he was fairly certain what would end up happening, and how could he go there when he wasn't prepared to be seen out with her?

He scrolled through his texts. He'd chatted with his dad earlier in the week. He was hopeful that they were getting close—that, if things went well, it would all be over soon. Zack could only hope. He felt like that whole situation had stolen too many years of his life already. He couldn't allow it to steal his chance at getting to know Maria—of having a relationship with her.

"I'm done," she called.

He picked up the sodas and took them through to the living room where she was sitting cross-legged on the sofa.

She smiled. "Sorry about that. I'd told Angel to call me about tonight."

"Do you want to go?"

She held her hands up. "Do you?"

He sat down on the sofa beside her and put his arm around her shoulders. "I'd rather stay here with you." She smiled up at him, but he shook his head. "That's what I'd like to do, but I'm not sure it's what we should do."

She nodded. "I had a feeling you were going to say that, but what I don't understand is why."

"Because it wouldn't be right to … to do what we could do here, when I can't take you out in public." He shook his head. "That seems wrong to me. You deserve more than that."

She gave him a rueful smile. "I appreciate that, but I'm not sure I agree."

"What do you mean?"

She chewed on her bottom lip for a moment, making him want to chew it for her. "I mean, you're a very private person. For some reason, which you can't explain, you don't want anyone to know that we're seeing each other. You're too much of a gentleman to think that you could, that we should … you know … without us being a bona fide couple first." She gave him a wicked smile. "If we were talking about someone else's situation, then I'd probably agree with you. But we're not. I get to have a say about what I want here, don't I?"

Zack nodded.

"Well, I think I want the private side of a relationship, even before we can have the public side."

His heart thundered in his chest. Was she saying what he thought she was?

She looked a little shamefaced. "Is that too brazen of me?"

"No! I don't think so." He gave her a half smile. "Come on, I'm the guy here. I'm trying to think of what's best for you."

She smiled. "I think I know what's best for me. You don't want people to know we're together—they don't have to know. But we can still *be* together, behind closed doors."

He cocked his head to one side. He would never have made her a proposition like that, but now she was suggesting it—how could he say no?

She leaned her head on his shoulder and looked up into his eyes. "Unless you don't want to?"

He ran his hand down her throat and trailed his fingers between her breasts. He'd love to show her how much he wanted to—right here and now. "I want to," he breathed.

"Then let's." She smiled and sat up. "But you're going to have to tell me how it has to work when we're out with our friends."

Zack pulled himself together. She was right. They should go out tonight, hang out with the gang like they would normally. How hard was that going to be after this afternoon? How hard would he be, knowing the whole time that he was going to take her home afterward and ... not just drop her off and say goodnight? "If we do this, we have to be the same as we've always been around our friends. To anyone else, it needs to look like we're just friends."

She nodded. "Okay. I can do that. I'm glad you're not the flirty kind. I don't think I could watch you chat up other women, but you don't usually do that, anyway."

He dropped a kiss on her plump, soft lips. "And now you know why."

A big smile spread across her face. "No. I don't. Tell me why?"

"I don't flirt with other women, because the woman I've wanted since I first came here is always right there. I don't flirt, because I'm only interested in one woman, and I haven't been able to flirt with you."

She smiled. "You can now."

"No. I can't. I ... I don't want to draw any attention to you as being someone that I care about."

She frowned. "Can you at least give me some kind of clue what's going on with you?"

"Yeah." It was only fair. They were at the beginning of something—hopefully something very special. He wanted her to have an idea of what he was dealing with; he just didn't want her to know anything specific—the less she knew, the better, for her own sake. "I ... I managed to make an enemy a few years ago. That's why I've lived around so much. It's why I didn't think I'd stay at Summer Lake too long. That enemy swore to track me down. He managed it a few times, early on. But I've moved three times since he last found me. I'd like to think the threat is over, but it won't ever really be over until ... until he's dealt with. I don't usually stay anywhere too long so that he can't find me. And I don't get close to people so that he can't threaten to hurt them to get to me. That's why I can't—won't—ask you to go out with me and start up a normal relationship in a normal way. If we did that, and he found me, then he'd no doubt find you, too. And I won't take that risk." When he finished speaking, he took hold of her hand and looked into her eyes. "I'm sorry. I should have told you all of that from the very beginning, before we even got as far as we have. I don't want to put you at risk—and you might think it's not worth taking the chance. If you want to walk away right now, I'll understand."

She cupped his face between her hands, and for a moment, he thought that was exactly what she was going to do—that she was going to tell him that she liked him, but she didn't want to get involved.

Instead, she smiled. "Don't be silly. I don't want to walk away. I'm glad you told me. Now I know why we have to be careful. And now I understand you a little bit better—I know you a little bit better, and that makes me happy."

"You're not afraid?"

She shook her head. "No. I trust you. I don't know what kind of bad people you got mixed up with, but you're not a bad person, are you?"

He shook his head.

"And they're not right in coming after you, are they?"

Zack hesitated. "If I were in his shoes, I might feel the same way he does. No. I'd never be in his shoes, because I'd never have done what he did in the first place."

"Can you tell me what happened? Why he's after you?"

"Maybe. One day soon. But not now." He felt like he'd burdened her with enough for one night.

"Okay. I'm glad you told me as much as you have." She smiled. "So, we should probably go tonight. People will think it's weird if neither of us shows up. That'd be more likely to give us away than showing up together as friends would."

He smiled and let his gaze run over her, sending a thrill through his veins at the thought that, if things went the way they seemed to be going, he'd get to do so much more than look at her later tonight. "As long as I can keep myself in check."

She waggled her eyebrows at him. "This could be fun. I can tease you, and we'll be the only ones who know what's going on." She smiled. "We can be together and keep it a secret that only we know."

His heart buzzed in his chest. How had he gotten this lucky? Not only did she understand, and not mind, but she wanted to make a game out of it. "Only until this is over. I want to take you out properly, I want to show you off, as my girl."

She smiled. "I love that idea, too, but for now, we can make the most of what is. Hiding isn't ideal—but that doesn't mean we can't make it fun."

~ ~ ~

Maria looked around as they entered the restaurant. She felt as though everyone must know that she'd spent the afternoon with Zack at his place and what they'd been up to. Well, to be fair, they hadn't gotten up to too much. They'd kissed—a lot. He was the best kisser! But he'd been a gentleman, so far. She was hoping she might get the chance to change that later. Kenzie waved at her from the behind the bar.

Zack stood a little closer to her and spoke under his breath. "It might not be that easy to hide with Kenzie around."

"Yeah. She was onto us at lunchtime." Maria had been okay to go along with hiding what was happening between them while they were sitting in his house earlier. The thought of someone looking for him and wanting to hurt him—and maybe her as well, as a way to get to him—had seemed so far-fetched, it'd been easy to dismiss it. Now, a little shiver ran down her spine. She looked up at him. "Is this going to make life more difficult for you?"

He held her gaze for a long moment. "Honestly? Yes, I'm going to be beating myself up the whole time. I'm already telling myself I'm a selfish asshole for not keeping the way I feel to myself. I shouldn't be putting you in this position, and if I had the self-discipline, I should stay away from you."

She had to smile. "You're not a selfish asshole. In fact, you should feel good that you put me out of my misery."

He gave her a puzzled look. "What misery?"

"I told you. I've liked you this whole time, too, and I was miserable wondering why I kept tormenting myself with the belief that you liked me, too. When you obviously didn't, or you would have done something about it."

He smiled. "Well, now you know. I like you a lot." He glanced over her shoulder. "But I'm going to do my best not to let anyone else know it."

She smiled. "It's easier for me."

"Why's that?"

"I can slip up and it doesn't matter if I like you, does it? I can just be that chick with a crush."

He shrugged. "I think we should both play it cool. Starting now. Angel and Luke are just behind you, heading this way."

"Okay, but I should warn you. Angel knows I like you."

He brushed his hand over the small of her back as she turned to greet their friends, sending shivers down her spine as he spoke quietly next to her ear. "Luke knows I like you, too."

That made her feel warm inside. She knew he and Luke were close; it made her happy that he'd told his friend the way he felt about her. It made it seem more real.

"Hey guys," Angel greeted them with a big smile. "I'm glad you're both here. What did you get up to today? I know you didn't go for a hike. Not with the rain we had."

Maria's heart started to race. She'd said she was okay with hiding from their friends, but until now, she hadn't considered that it would mean lying to them. She didn't like to tell lies; it wasn't in her nature. She shrugged. "Not much. I watched a movie." That wasn't a lie.

"I did, too." She had to smile at the sound of Zack's voice beside her. She didn't dare turn to look at him, though.

"Hey, everyone!" Roxy appeared out of the crowd. "How are we?"

Maria laughed. "Good, thanks. How are you? How was your head this morning?"

Roxy rolled her eyes. "I was grateful for your suggestion to put a glass of water and some aspirin on the nightstand, put it that way. I hope I wasn't too embarrassing last night?"

Maria smiled. She was hardly going to remind her friend about the way she'd set her up to go home with Zack—though at some point she did want to thank her.

Luke laughed. "No, you just had one too many. You were fun. Unlike Angel and Maria who, for a minute there, made me think the zombie apocalypse was here."

"Hey!" Angel pushed at his arm. "That's not nice."

Zack chuckled. "Maybe not, but he does have a point. This one," he nudged Maria with his elbow, "almost bludgeoned me to death with a towel rail."

"What's that?" Colt had come to join them and gave Maria an enquiring look. "Did he just say what I think he did?"

Maria smiled. She liked Colt. He wasn't her type, but he was a good-looking guy. He was one of their group of friends, though he didn't get out as much as the rest of them. As deputy sheriff, he tended to work a lot of unsociable hours. "Yes, but it's not as bad as it sounds. I promise. You don't need to arrest me for attempted assault or anything."

Colt laughed. "Don't worry, I didn't plan to." He gave Zack a look she didn't understand. "But I might recruit you to the local defense force if ever things get hairy around here."

Maria risked a look at Zack. It seemed he and Colt were having a conversation with their eyes. She'd have to ask him about it later.

"Are we going to grab a table?" asked Roxy. "We need to lay claim to one soon, or we'll be standing all night."

"That's what I came to tell you," said Colt. "Austin and Logan have snagged us a table right by the band."

Maria shot a look at Roxy who tried to look innocent but failed miserably.

"Lead the way, Rox," said Zack. "I'm sure Logan will be pleased to see you."

Roxy shot him an evil look. "Button it, Mr. Aguila, if you don't mind."

Zack just laughed. "I don't know what your problem is. You know what he's like. I'm sure he'd be more than happy to oblige you."

Roxy shook her head. "Don't! I'm serious. I'm not interested in a romp with Logan, and that's all he thinks women are made for. I find him nice to look at, that's all." She shot a look at Maria. "And I don't know why you're ribbing me for having a secret crush on someone. I could start on you if you're not careful."

Zack held a hand up. "Okay, okay. Sorry. I was only teasing you. Let me buy you a drink to make up for it."

Roxy grinned at him. "Oh, okay then, if you insist."

Once he and Luke had gone to the bar, Maria and the girls sat down at the table. Austin and Logan greeted them, and Maria had to smile to herself. If she wanted to hide how she felt about Zack, she'd do well to take lessons from Roxy. She had this big crush on Logan, but you'd never guess it from the way she talked to him. The way she talked about him when he wasn't there was a different matter altogether. But watching her greet him and ask him about work, you'd think he was merely a co-worker, and one she barely tolerated.

Angel leaned in and spoke quietly. "Are you hiding something?"

Maria shook her head. She desperately wanted to tell her friend what was happening, but this wasn't her secret. It was Zack's. She'd have to talk to him about it. He obviously trusted Luke enough to tell him that he liked her, she hoped he'd be okay with her talking to Angel about him—she needed to have a girlfriend to share with.

Chapter Six

Zack leaned back in his chair and watched the girls dance. Mostly, he watched Maria's ass dance, but he couldn't help it. And it wasn't as though it was anything that would give away his interest in her—he'd never been able to hide his interest in that ass.

He frowned as Logan leaned over and gave him a lecherous grin as he pointed his bottle toward Maria's rear end. "What I wouldn't give ..."

Zack sucked in a deep breath. He was protective of all the girls. He often reminded Logan that he should be a bit more respectful, but right now, he didn't feel like being the voice of reason. He felt more like landing his fist in the middle of Logan's face.

Logan sat back. Even though Zack hadn't moved, he must have given off a wave of anger or something that had made his thoughts clear.

Logan held up a hand. "Sorry, bro. I forgot. You have a sweet spot for our Maria, don't you?"

Damn. On his first night of trying to hide how he felt about her, he was already making it obvious.

Luke came to his rescue. "It's not about having a sweet spot for anyone. It's about having a bit of respect for everyone. You're talking about a friend; she's not a piece of meat."

Logan held his hands up apologetically. "I know. Sorry. You're right. I think I've played the game so long, that it's hard to see it as anything more than a game—and the players as more than pieces." He chuckled and added. "Of ass."

Zack shook his head at him. "You were doing well there. I almost thought you were sincere."

"I was. I am. I just can't resist saying the line when I see it. I don't mean any harm. You know that. I just like to have fun—but only with girls who are looking for that kind of fun. I'd never …" He shook his head. "Sorry, guys, I was only having a laugh."

Zack gave him a rueful smile. "You're fine. I just get a bit protective."

Logan rolled his eyes. "Tell me something I don't know. The rumors about you being from some kind of mafia family didn't get started for nothing, you know. Even if I wanted to make a move on Maria, I wouldn't dare. You're like the big brother mafioso."

Zack tried to laugh it off, but it made him wonder. Had he always been more protective—too protective of Maria because of the way he felt about her? Had he been giving himself away without even knowing it?

Luke caught his eye. "Yeah, he's like a big brother to all of them."

Logan pursed his lips. "Kind of, but especially Maria. We all knew you had a thing for Angel. And Roxy … well, Roxy's something else."

Zack was eager to shift the focus away to himself. He smiled. "What about Roxy?"

Logan laughed. "She wouldn't even give me the time of day, let alone anything else."

Luke smirked at Zack. "Are you sure about that?"

"Damned sure. She's not that kind of girl. She'd shut me down in a heartbeat."

"I think she would if you tried your usual approach with her—she's not going to fall into bed with you," said Zack, "but what about, if you asked her out?"

Logan looked at him as if he'd gone crazy. "Asked her out?" He laughed. "You do know this is me you're talking to, right? I don't ask women out. I ask them if they want to sleep with me."

"Why, though?" asked Austin who was sitting on the other side of him.

Logan shrugged and took a swig of his beer. "Because who needs the hassle?"

Zack laughed. "Spoken like a true commitment-phobe."

Logan grinned at him. "It takes one to know one."

Zack shrugged. He wasn't afraid of commitment—at least, not for its own sake, but if Logan and anyone else wanted to believe that about him, that was fine—and might actually be a good thing.

They all looked up as the girls came back from the dance floor. Angel came and sat on Luke's knee and landed a kiss on his lips. Zack had to avoid looking at Maria. He wished that she could do the same to him.

Roxy sat down next to Colt with a smile. "What's going on in your world, officer?" she asked. "Anything interesting? Any crime sprees we need to be aware of?"

Colt shook his head. "This is Summer Lake … there's rarely anything too bad going on."

Zack nodded. He was glad of it.

Roxy shrugged. "One day there'll be something mega-exciting."

Zack hoped not.

"But in the meantime," Roxy turned to Austin. "What about you? Anyone new and interesting moved to town lately?"

Austin shrugged. As a realtor he would know about new people moving to town, but he didn't look comfortable with the question. "You know I don't like to talk about newcomers or who's buying and selling."

Logan grinned at him. "Only because you want to get to know the new chicks before anyone else knows they're here."

Colt blew out a sigh. "Not everyone thinks like you do, Logan."

Logan grinned at Roxy. Maybe he was looking for sympathy, but he didn't get any from her. She looked at Austin instead. "Does he mean that there are some new girls moved to town?"

Austin nodded, and looked uncomfortable.

Zack raised an eyebrow at him. "You don't like them?"

Colt laughed. "He likes one of them a little too much. And Nadia is not happy about it."

Zack gave Austin a sympathetic smile. Austin had been seeing Nadia for as long as Zack had been here, but what Zack couldn't figure out was why. She was one of those high-maintenance, pretty, but picky girls—the kind Zack didn't have any time for.

"Who are they?" asked Maria.

"They're sisters. Amber and Jade. Their grandma runs the post office—Lenny."

"Oh. Lenny's lovely," said Maria. "She's told me about her granddaughters before. She adores them. She must be so happy that they're here."

"You haven't heard?" asked Colt. "Lenny had a heart attack. Amber and Jade have come to help out. Jade's going to run the post office and Amber's going to be taking care of Lenny."

"Oh, no. I didn't know. Is Lenny in the hospital or is she home? I'd like to go and see her."

"She's still in the hospital," said Austin.

Zack wanted to put his arm around Maria's shoulders. She looked upset at the news. It didn't surprise him. That was the way she was. He wouldn't have even known the name of the woman who worked at the post office. Maria knew who she was, knew about her granddaughters and obviously cared about her.

"She's going to be okay." Austin gave Maria a reassuring smile. "They said she should be able to come home by the end of next week."

Logan smirked at him. "Who said that—and how do you know?"

Austin shook his head. "Amber told me, when I talked to her earlier about the apartment they're renting."

"And does Nadiaa know that you talked to Amber earlier?"

Austin rolled his eyes. "Can we change the subject? There's nothing going on, and Nadia's ..." He shrugged. Zack willed Logan not to say what he knew at least half the people around the table were thinking—that Nadia was a bitch.

Maria smiled brightly around at everyone. "We should change the subject and we should get you guys up and dancing. Come on. We're supposed to be out for a good time, not to sit around gossiping. She got her feet and grabbed Zack's hand. "Roxy, see if you can get Austin onto the dance floor."

Roxy grinned and dragged him to his feet. "It'll do you good," she said with a smile. "I might not be a precious gem, but at least you know Nadia's not going to mind if she hears you were dancing with me."

Zack saw that Angel had gone to get Colt up. That made him smile. These girls tried so hard to make sure no one was left out. His smile faded as Maria looped her arms around his neck and looked up into his eyes.

"Sorry," she said. "I hope this is okay, but I figured everyone needed to get away from that conversation and I had to come up with something to get my hands on you again."

Zack laughed as he closed his arms around her. "This is more than okay. It's perfect."

She pressed herself a little closer against him, making heat rush through his veins. "Not quite perfect," she said with a smile, "but a little closer to it than we were."

He pursed his lips. What he really wanted to do was lower them to hers and kiss her. Then take her home, take her to bed—and see how close to perfect they could get. Instead, he drew in a deep breath and let it out slowly. Then he gritted his teeth when someone tapped his shoulder and he turned to see Logan grinning at him.

"My turn. Until we get a few more ladies around to even up the numbers, you're going to have to share."

Zack's arm's tightened instinctively around Maria. He wanted to tell Logan where he could go. Why couldn't he cut in on Austin and dance with Roxy?

Maria smiled up at him. "He's right," she said. "It's only fair."

Zack's hand balled into fists as he walked back to the table where Luke gave him a worried look when he sat down. "Cool it, would you? You won't fool anyone acting like that."

Zack shrugged. Right now, he didn't care about fooling anyone into thinking that he and Maria were just friends. He was more interested in telling the whole world that she was his—and that Logan, and every other guy had better keep their hands off.

"Calm down," said Luke. "What's she going to think when she sees you storming off like that?"

Zack shrugged, and the adrenaline started to recede. "She knows. She knows how I feel. I couldn't keep it up. We spent the day together."

"Together, together?"

He nodded.

"But ... I thought ... last night you said you liked her, but you couldn't do anything about it. What changed?"

Zack had to smile. "My resolve finally crumbled. I can't not do something about it. I mean," he turned his head to watch her dancing with Logan, "look at her. I drove her home last night and it was all I could do to drive away when I dropped her off. Today, we had lunch and we got to talking and ..." He shrugged again. "I spent the afternoon with her."

"And now what? Now you're together? It didn't look that way, at least, not until Logan cut in on you."

"That's because it can't look that way. I shouldn't be doing this. I told you last night. I shouldn't let myself get close to her."

"Why?" Luke was such an easy-going guy, but he was obviously frustrated.

"My past. It's going to find me one day, and when it does, anyone I'm close to is going to be in danger."

Luke shook his head. "So, what are you doing? Was this afternoon a one-off?"

"No. We're going to start seeing each other—but to everyone else, we're just going to be friends."

"And you think you'll be able to keep it a secret?"

"I was hoping so." Maria had joked earlier about not wanting to see him flirting with other women, what he hadn't considered was how he would react to other men hitting on her. To be fair, Logan wasn't hitting on her. They were friends and Logan was just being Logan. But still. Zack had wanted to take him by the throat. How would he react if some stranger was hitting on her?

Luke raised his eyebrows. "Good luck with that."

"Thanks. I think I'm going to need it."

~ ~ ~

Maria hugged Angel and Roxy. "I'll catch up with you in the week, ladies."

"What about me?" asked Logan.

She laughed. "I'll see you when I see you." She turned to Zack who was already standing a few feet away, ready to go. "Sorry to keep you waiting; are you sure you don't mind giving me a ride?"

"It's not a problem, it's on my way." He did such a good job of seeming casual, she had to wonder if maybe he wasn't as eager to get out of here as she was.

"I can take you later if you want to stay a while," said Logan.

Maria forced a smile. Logan was a sweetie, but he'd gotten in the way so much tonight, it almost felt like he was doing it on purpose. "Thanks, but I'm pooped. I'm ready to go now and since Zack's leaving anyway ..." She shrugged.

Luke gave her a knowing smile, making her think that Zack must have told him. "You get on home. Get to bed."

She felt her cheeks color. Had Zack told him that was the plan? "Yeah. Goodnight." She caught up to Zack and he started toward the doors without a word.

Once they were outside in the fresh air, she looked up at him. "Are you okay?"

"I am. Are you?"

She nodded. "That was more of a minefield than I expected."

"Wasn't it? Since when has Logan been so into you?"

She let out a small laugh. "Never. He isn't, but I will say he has the worst timing. I was so pleased when I managed to get you on the dance floor and then he came and spoiled it."

Zack smiled as they reached the truck and he opened the passenger door for her. "I'm glad you thought he spoiled it, too. I had to walk away before I did something stupid. I didn't want to let him near you."

A warm feeling spread though her chest. "You did? I thought you were just playing along with it—looking relieved to be able to get off the dance floor."

He shook his head. "No. What I was feeling couldn't have been further from relief."

She climbed up into the truck and smiled down at him. "What were you feeling?"

He held her gaze for a long moment and then closed the door without a word. Butterflies swirled in her stomach as he walked around to the driver's side and then got in and leaned on the center console. "I felt jealous and possessive. I know that's crazy, and I know I have no right to feel that way, but that's the truth. I wanted to shove him away from you, and I wanted to tell him and the rest of the world that you're mine."

Maria's heart pounded in her chest. She didn't like guys who behaved that way. She wasn't into big macho men who thought they owned their women, but when Zack said she was his, it set her heart racing. She loved the idea!

"Does that make me an asshole?"

She laughed. "No. It should. I don't like jealous men, but I have to tell you, knowing you feel that way about me ..." She shuddered as a shiver ran down her spine. "I ..." She'd been about to tell him how much it turned her on, but she thought better of it. She was trying to be as straightforward as possible with him, but that seemed just a little too brazen. "I like it," she said instead.

He leaned toward her and she lifted her lips to meet his. It was the briefest kiss, but it turned her insides to mush. "We should get you home."

She was surprised when he turned into her street. She'd assumed they go back to his place.

He brought the truck to a stop in the same spot he'd parked in last night. "I think you know that I'd like nothing more than to come inside."

She swallowed and made herself focus on the safer meaning of those words. She nodded, and then it hit her. He wasn't even going to do that—he was dropping her off. She searched his face. "Did something change?"

He reached over and took hold of her hand. "No, nothing changed. I still want this. I want you." The way he looked at her, left no doubt of that. "But I need you to be sure first.

Tonight was tougher on me than I expected. I think it was for you, too?"

She couldn't deny it. She hadn't enjoyed lying to her friends. The reality of keeping what they were doing a secret was much less appealing than the idea of it. She nodded. "It's not going to be easy."

"I know, so, before we go somewhere that you might regret. I want you to take the time to think about it."

She squeezed his hand. "I wouldn't regret it, Zack." She smiled and dropped her gaze. "I've thought about it ever since that first night when I gave you a ride back over here from Four Mile."

His lips twitched into a smile. "You thought about it that night, too?"

She nodded.

"I had the toughest time not making a move on you."

"Why didn't you?"

He held her gaze. "Because if I had—if we had—that's all it would ever have been. I knew even then that you were someone I wanted to have in my life—even if it could only be as a friend."

She leaned toward him and landed a kiss on his lips. "I want you in my life, Zack, and not just as a friend."

"That's easy to say, but I want you to take some time and think about it. Think about the bad side of tonight. Think how difficult this could be. I don't know how long we'd have to hide it. And honestly, I need to think about whether I can live with myself."

She frowned at him. "What do you mean?"

"I mean, I promised myself I would never, ever put you at risk. If we do this, no matter how careful we are, there's going to be a risk."

"I don't care."

He smiled and smoothed a strand of hair away from her face. "You should. Promise me you'll think about it?"

She nodded sadly. "Okay."

"Don't think I don't want this. It's going to kill me to drive away from here tonight, but I think we need to cool off. Make a rational decision in the cold hard light of day—not a rushed one fueled by desire."

All the muscles in her stomach and lower tightened. He desired her. She knew he did. She desired him, too. She was fairly certain that she could persuade him to ignore his better judgment and come inside with her if she tried. She was also certain that she wasn't going to change her mind about this. She'd hoped for so long that the two of them might get together. Nothing—not even some murky threat from his past—was going to deter her now. "Okay, then. How long do you want me to think it over?"

He smiled. "Call me?"

She laughed. "I'd be calling you before you even made it home."

"Do you have plans for tomorrow?"

"Just waiting for you to call me."

He touched her cheek. "I will."

Chapter Seven

The next morning, Maria was awake by seven-thirty—so much for getting to sleep in on her weekend off. She hadn't slept well at all. She'd tossed and turned all night, thinking about Zack and about what they could be doing if he'd come in with her, or she'd gone home with him. She sat up in bed and leaned back against the pillows. If she wanted to find the bright side, and she almost always did, she could smile at the fact that having spent the last two nights thinking about what might happen between them, she was high on anticipation. She hugged the duvet tight to her chest and felt her nipples stiffen.

Her whole body seemed to be humming with pent up desire. She wasn't above taking care of that herself. A girl had to do what she had to do—especially when she'd been single for a long while. She didn't want to relieve the ache between her legs herself though. She was aching for Zack and she knew that the longer she had to wait, the better it would feel when he finally gave her what she wanted.

She got out of bed wishing that she'd told him she would call him first thing this morning. Instead, she'd have to wait until whenever he called her. He'd said he would, and she didn't

doubt him, but she hated not knowing when it would be—
how long she'd have to wait.

She'd tried to do as he'd asked and think seriously about
whether she was prepared to deal with the reality of what they
were doing. She already knew that however tough it might be,
it was worth it. When she was younger, one of her uncles had
had an affair. She'd listened to her mother and aunts talk about
it when he was discovered. The other woman had been a
neighbor, and apparently, it had gone on for years. She'd
wondered at the time how they'd managed to keep it a secret
and how it must feel to sneak around like that, lying to people.
That was exactly what she was planning to do with Zack.
Granted, they weren't cheating on anyone. Them seeing each
other wasn't hurting anyone. But from what Zack had said, if
this enemy of his found him and found out that they were
seeing each other, he might hurt her. She shook her head. She
couldn't take that seriously. She knew she should, but it just
couldn't penetrate the layers of desire and excitement that were
making her head feel fuzzy.

She went downstairs and made herself some coffee. She
smiled when she remembered the croissants he'd brought her
yesterday—a whole box of them. That was so sweet of him.
She wouldn't have expected him to know what her favorite
anything was, but it proved that he'd been paying attention to
her while she'd thought he just saw her as a friend.

She grabbed her phone when it rang and smiled when she
saw his name on the display.

"Good morning."

"Good morning, beautiful." She could hear the smile in his
voice. "Is it too early?"

She laughed. "No. I was sitting here by the phone waiting and hoping—and eating croissants to distract myself."

He chuckled. "You're eating croissants? In your PJs?"

"Uh-huh. Don't worry, I'll save you some—you brought me enough of them."

He laughed. "I don't mind if you eat them all by yourself—as long as I can watch."

"Watch?"

"Yeah." His voice sounded deeper, gruffer somehow, and she knew that he was thinking naughty thoughts. Though why croissants would have that effect on him she had no idea. "Why?"

He sighed, and her scalp tingled at the sound of it. "Because, Maria *mía*, you make it so damned obvious how much you enjoy them. You let yourself go and it makes me …"

She swallowed. Angel had teased her before that she made sex noises when she ate those croissants—they were just so damned good. "Makes you what?" she breathed.

"It makes me hard. It makes me want you even more."

"Oh." She didn't know what else to say. She knew what she wanted, though. "Why don't you come over, then? I just made a pot of coffee and there are plenty of croissants left."

She could almost hear his internal struggle. "Did you think about what this means? Are you sure you want to do this?"

She laughed. "I did, and I want to do it. I'm too tempted to think straight right now, but when I was thinking straight, when I accepted that this will not be easy, and that it might even be dangerous, I still wanted it. I want you Zack. I want there to be an us."

"You're sure?"

She laughed. "Yes. How many ways do you want me to say it? Oh, I know what will help to convince you. I'm going to start eating another croissant right now."

He chuckled. "I'm on my way."

Zack parked on the street in front of her house and looked around as he walked up the path to the front door. He couldn't see anyone around, though that was hardly surprising at nine o'clock on a Sunday morning. The little hairs on the back of his neck stood up at the thought that someone could be around—someone could be watching him—and he wouldn't know. Just because he'd dashed over here at the thought of getting to see Maria eat her croissants, he couldn't afford to get careless. He couldn't let his desire for her make him forget. He had a feeling he knew where things were about to go between them—he couldn't hold out for much longer, and it sounded like Maria didn't want to hold out at all. But they had other business to take care of today as well. He was going to be here for the next week. He wanted to see as much of her as he could in that time, but he wanted to come up with a plausible reason for them to spend a lot of time together.

He knocked on the door and had to bite the inside of his lip when she opened it. She was still in her pajamas. Her long black hair was tied up in a messy pony tail—and she had a half-eaten croissant in her hand.

She greeted him with a smile. "That didn't take you long."

He chuckled. "I got here as fast as I could. I wasn't joking when I said I want to watch you eat that."

She held the door open and stood back for him to come in. "I thought I'd be starting another one just for you by the time you get here. Do you want one of your own and a coffee?"

"Just a coffee for me, thanks." He followed her through to the kitchen and perched on a stool at the counter while she poured him a coffee.

She set it down in front of him with a smile. "I'm glad you called early. I was dreading spending the day waiting and wondering."

"I should have left it until later, given you more time to think this over …"

She shook her head with a smile. "I spent most of the night thinking about it. I didn't want to. I already knew what my answer would be, but I promised you I'd think about it, so I did. I know it's going to be difficult and I know there might be some risk involved. But," she smiled and put her hands on his knees, "I think you're worth it."

He took hold of her hands and drew her closer until she was standing between his legs and his arms were closed around her. "I'll do my best to be worth it."

She laughed and reached for her croissant. "I'm hoping that if I keep eating this, you'll at least make it worth my while."

A wave of heat surged through his veins, and his cock sprang to life. He wanted to tell her that there was no rush to go there, but he couldn't make himself speak.

She gave him a wicked smile and took a bite of the croissant and gave a satisfied little moan. "Oh, God. That's so good."

He watched her lips move as she chewed slowly. "You are a wicked woman. And I thought you were so sweet."

She chuckled and sucked the tip of her finger. "What's wicked about enjoying my breakfast?"

He put his hands on her hips and drew her closer again. "Nothing, as long as you understand that it makes me want you for breakfast."

She nodded. "I understand." She put the pastry down and looped her arms up around his neck. "That's what I want, too."

He couldn't hold out. He dropped his head to kiss her and slid his hands around to finally hold her amazing ass. She let out another little moan when he started to squeeze.

He lifted his head. "Better than croissants?" he asked with a smile.

She laughed. "Not yet, but you're only just getting started, right?"

He smiled through pursed lips and slid down from the stool, picking her up and setting her in his place. All his intentions of taking things slowly flew out the window. He wanted her, and he wanted her now.

She looked up at him. Her eyes were filled with a mixture of desire and trust. It made him even harder to know that she felt that way about him. He put his hands on her shoulders, then slid them up to cup the sides of her neck. "I am just getting started—*we* are just getting started, but I need you to tell me one more time that you're sure."

She nodded. Her breath was coming slowly. He couldn't resist watching her heavy breasts rise and fall. "I'm sure."

He smiled and stepped between her legs, keeping a little distance between them at first. He slid his fingers up into her hair and pulled her head back. Her plump, pink lips begged for him to taste them, and he did. He started out slowly, but once he slid his tongue into her mouth and she opened up for him, he was lost. He leaned into her, pressing his aching cock into the heat between her legs. She grasped his shoulders tight and moaned into his mouth, making him drop his hands to grasp her ass and rock his hips against her.

She wrapped her legs around his and clamped him to her as she moved in time with him. She felt so good, but it wasn't enough. He wanted more. He needed to be inside her.

He lifted his head and looked down into her eyes. She was panting now, her eyes wide with desire. "Please don't tease me anymore, Zack. I want this. I want you."

He closed his eyes for a moment, wanting to throw her down right there on the kitchen floor and give her what she wanted. "Show me where."

She slid down from the stool, took his hand and led him up the stairs. His cock was throbbing, desperate to be out of his jeans and inside her. He closed the door behind them and then pressed her up against it.

There was nothing shy or hesitant about the way she tugged at the bottom of his T-shirt. He helped out, tugging it up and off. He thrust his hard-on between her legs as she ran her hands over his bare chest.

"I can't believe you're in here." She smiled at him. "I don't mind telling you that I've dreamed about this."

He closed his hands around her breasts and then dropped his head to mouth each nipple in turn, drawing more of those little sighs and moans from her. "I don't mind telling you that I've dreamed about this, too."

She chuckled. "So, let's make each other's dreams come true."

He didn't need telling twice. While she tugged at his zipper and pushed his jeans down, he slid his hands inside her top and teased her nipples between his fingers.

She moaned again and slid her hand inside his boxers. His breath caught in his throat as she closed her fingers around him and began to stroke up and down the length of him. "Does that feel good?"

He nodded and twisted the now stiff peaks of her nipples between his fingers, making her gasp. "Does that?"

"Yes!" she breathed.

He hated to let go, but he had to see her naked. He stepped back out of her grasp and slid her pajama bottoms down. She was as eager as he was and pulled her top off then leaned back against the door. He pushed his boxers down and kicked out of them and his jeans without taking his eyes off her.

"I'm not small."

He met her gaze. "You're perfect."

She smiled. "Thank you. So are you."

He leaned his weight against her and closed his eyes as his aching cock pressed into the heat between her legs. All that was keeping them apart was the cotton of her panties and it wouldn't be able to keep him out for long. He reached down and slid his finger inside. She was hot and wet, and she moaned again when he traced his finger over her entrance. She rocked her hips and rubbed herself against his hand. He'd only intended to see if she was ready, but the way she moved so eagerly made him want to give her more. He teased her clit and she moaned loudly and bit into his shoulder.

"Please, Zack." The way she said it made him ache.

"Please, what?" He moved his hand faster and slid a finger inside her. "Is this better?"

Her eyes glazed with pleasure, and she leaned her head back against the door, panting and moaning as he worked her.

She reached out and closed her fingers around him, but he moved away. He wanted to focus on her first. He kissed her deeply and she clung to him, it was all he could do not spread her legs. Instead, he dropped to his knees and pulled her panties down, then nuzzled his face between her legs.

Her fingers tangled in his hair. "Oh, God. Zack."

He flicked his tongue over her. She tasted so sweet. He held her open and sank his tongue inside. Her thighs clenched around him and her flesh quivered under his touch as he sucked and tasted, taking her to the edge. She was rocking her hips and moaning. He knew what she needed. He leaned back and looked up into her eyes as he licked his fingers and then sucked them. Her lips moved, but only a needy little sound came out. He smiled and rested his fingers at her entrance while he returned his attention to her clit, taking the little bud between his lips and sucking hard. He felt her tense and thrust his fingers deep inside her, moving faster and faster until she screamed, and her inner muscles clenched around him, gripping him tightly as she rocked desperately in time with him. He sucked harder. Loving the taste of her as she let go.

When she stilled, he slowly withdrew his fingers and looked up into her eyes. She was flushed and panting, and she'd never looked more beautiful. "You well and truly finished me off."

He smiled and got to his feet. "No, I've only just warmed you up." He led her to the bed and lay her down on it. "We're just getting started."

Maria licked her lips as he lay down beside her.

"When you said you wanted me, did you mean you wanted my fingers?"

She shook her head—though she might have, if she'd known what they could do.

"Did you mean you wanted my mouth on you?"

She shook her head again—though she'd never refuse the offer, now she knew how talented his lips and tongue were.

He propped himself up on one elbow and looked down into her eyes as his fingers closed around her breast. "What did you mean?"

She swallowed. He wanted her to say it? She reached down and touched him, enjoying the way his eyes closed for a moment and he drew in a deep breath.

"What do you want?"

She smiled. "I want this."

He rocked his hips. "Like this? You want my cock in your hand?"

She shook her head. There was no point being shy with him now. If he wanted to hear it, she'd be happy to tell him. "I want your cock inside me. I want you to fuck me, Zack." Even as she said it, she could feel him get hotter and harder in her hand.

He positioned himself above her and she spread her legs wide. "I want to be inside you. I want to bury my cock inside your hot, wet pussy."

She nodded. Understanding now how the words added to the pleasure.

"I want to fuck you." The tip of him was pressing at her entrance, hot and hard.

She writhed under him needing him to do it. She was making those noises again. She couldn't help it. She moaned as she lifted her hips, needing him to make good on his words. "Do it," she gasped.

He gave her a half smile and pushed a little deeper. Enough to send waves of need crashing through her, but not enough to satisfy them.

"Please, Zack," she begged. "Fuck me."

He thrust his hips hard and she screamed as he filled her. He was so big, so hard. He filled her and stretched her with every thrust of his hips, driving deep inside her faster and faster. She wrapped her legs around him and clung on as he plundered her body and her mouth. She was powerless to resist him, and she didn't want to. He was claiming her, making her his, and all she could do was go with him as he pounded into her. With each thrust the tension was building inside her, mounting and mounting until she couldn't take any more. She grasped his shoulders tightly, sinking her nails into his skin as she screamed her release. He kept going, giving her no respite until he, too, tensed and found his release deep inside her. She saw stars as he carried her away on a wave of pleasure like she'd never known before. By the time they lay still she was spent. She hugged him close and ran her fingers through his hair.

He lifted his head and smiled at her tenderly. "Did we make any dreams come true?"

She chuckled. "No. I hadn't even dreamed it could be that good."

He planted a soft kiss on her lips. "Me neither. I had no idea."

Chapter Eight

There was no awkwardness between them afterward. That was something he'd been concerned about. She'd become such a good friend to him, he'd hate it if taking their friendship to a different level—the physical level—were to change the closeness he felt with her.

As she reheated the coffee and grinned at him, he knew he needn't have worried. "Well, I guess we've crossed that line now, haven't we? There's no going back."

He smiled. "I wouldn't want to. I've waited a long time for this."

She smiled happily. "Me, too. And I don't mind telling you that you were more than worth the wait."

"I'm glad I didn't disappoint you."

"I don't think you could if you tried." She came and set a fresh mug down in front of him.

He caught her arm and drew her to him. "You're amazing."

She chuckled. "Thank you, though I'd say you're the amazing one. You did most of the work. I just had to lie back and enjoy."

He landed a kiss on her lips. "You were hardly passive. In fact, I seem to remember you were quite vocal."

She hung her head. "Sorry, I can't help it. It's like the croissants. I don't know that I'm doing it, but when I'm enjoying something, I like to a make a noise about it, apparently."

He chuckled. "Don't ever apologize. I love it."

She gave him a wicked smile. "Yeah. I noticed that you like me being vocal."

"What do you mean?" he asked, but he had a feeling he already knew.

"You like me to tell you."

"Tell me what?"

She narrowed her eyes at him. "Are you trying to make me say it again?"

He winked at her. "Only if you want me to do it again." His cock was already starting to stir. She was right. It turned him on so much when she said it, when she told him she wanted his cock inside her—when she wanted him so badly that she begged him to give it to her.

She raised her eyebrows at him. "Right now?"

He nodded and let his gaze wander over her. "You don't want to?"

She nodded and ran her tongue over her bottom lip, making his cock stand to attention in a hurry. "Let me just …" She took the mugs over to the sink and turned the coffee-pot off. "We'll never get breakfast at this rate."

He followed her to the counter and slid his arms around her waist before she could turn around.

"Oh!" She looked back over her shoulder at him. "I thought you meant we should go back upstairs." He kissed the back of her neck, and keeping one arm around her waist, he slid her pajamas down with his other hand.

"Not necessarily," he breathed.

She rubbed her ass against him, torturing him through his jeans. He unfastened them and pushed them down in a hurry. "We could just stay right …" He slid his cock between her legs and pulled her back against him, "… here."

"Zack," she breathed and gripped the counter, leaning forward against it.

He cupped her ass cheeks with both hands and spread them wide.

"Fuck me, Zack."

Hearing her say it was all he needed. He held her hips back against him and thrust deep, loving the way she screamed as he buried himself inside her. She was so wet, so tight, he lost himself inside her as she pushed back against him, taking each thrust deep and hard. He reached around to touch her, wanting to make sure she was getting what she needed. It seemed she was as she moved frantically under him gasping and moaning as she took him deeper. He pulled back and looked down, almost taking himself over the edge as he watched himself pull out and then plunge inside her over and over. He rolled her clit between his finger and thumb and saw her knuckles whiten as she gripped the counter harder. "Oh, God! Fuck me, Zack!"

Her words took him over the edge, and he buried himself deep and let go. Her inner muscles clenched him tight, over and over again as her orgasm took her and he spilled his need deep inside her.

His legs felt like jelly when they finally straightened up. She turned around and looped her arms up around his neck. "Wow! I wasn't expecting that."

He brushed his lips over hers. "I wasn't either. But I think a little surprise is good every now and then."

She laughed. "Every now and then—or every day would be fine by me."

He held her close to his chest. Every day would be more than fine by him, too. But her words reminded him that that they had a lot to figure out. How could they be together every day without people noticing what was going on? And there was also this minor detail of him not being here all the time anyway. Clay had said they were free and clear until a week from Monday, but then they'd be flying him back to Nashville. His job meant that he and Luke flew Clay wherever he wanted to go, whenever he wanted to go. Fortunately, now that he was engaged to Marianne, Clay mostly wanted to be here at the lake, but Nashville was still home base.

Maria's smile had faded as she watched his face. "Did I say something wrong?"

"No." He dropped a kiss on her lips. "I love the idea of being able to do this with you every day. It's just that my mind got caught up in how to make that possible."

Maria couldn't help smiling to herself as she fixed them a drink later that afternoon. Today had been the perfect day, as far as she was concerned. They'd started out with a bang—literally—and then followed it up with dessert in the kitchen. Her tummy flipped over at the memory of how he'd taken her from behind this morning, up against the kitchen counter no less! She wouldn't consider herself to be prim and proper in the bedroom—but she was hardly very worldly, either. She chuckled at the thought—never mind the bedroom, she'd been completely inexperienced in the kitchen until this morning.

They'd showered and she'd gotten dressed after that and then they'd spent the day hanging out here. Even when she'd tried to make herself think seriously last night about what hiding their relationship would mean, she hadn't thought very deeply. She hadn't gotten as far as realizing that they wouldn't be able to do all things a normal couple would do. Like go out for a walk on the beach and hold hands or go to town and browse the stores or even go to lunch at the Boathouse. They'd done that yesterday, as friends, but Zack thought—and he was right—that they probably shouldn't do it two days in a row.

She looked up when he came to join her in the kitchen. "Can I do anything to help?"

"I was just bringing these back in. Are you going to be hungry? I know we can't go out, so I was starting to think about what I can make."

He came to her and closed his arms around her. "We can order something from Giuseppe's. We probably shouldn't go out, but I don't want you to have to cook."

"I don't mind. I like to cook on the weekends. I'm often too tired to bother in the week."

He looked sad.

"What's the matter?"

He planted a kiss on her forehead. "You have to go back to work tomorrow, don't you."

"Yeah. But you're still here for another week. At least it's not you going back to work."

He smiled. "Does it come naturally to you?"

"What?"

"Always finding the bright side?"

She shrugged. "It didn't used to. I used to spend a lot of my time worrying about things that might go wrong and seeing the worst in things. One day I realized that even though I can't control what happens, I can control the way I feel about it. If you look for the bright side you tend to be happy and hopeful, but if you look for the worst in things, you end up miserable. Since I can control how I feel most of the time, I choose to be happy as much as I can."

He rested his chin on top of her head. "I love that about you. You're just a little positive peanut."

She laughed and looked up at him. "Seriously? A peanut?"

He laughed. "Yeah, why not. It's cute—and you're cute."

She rolled her eyes. "If you say so. But come on, let's go and check out Giuseppe's menu. I'm getting hungry and it'll take them a while to deliver."

~ ~ ~

After they'd eaten pizza, Zack insisted that he should clean up. Maria had waited on him all day. She didn't seem to mind, but he didn't want her getting the idea that that was how he expected or wanted things to be.

She smiled at him when he came back into the living room with two glasses of wine. "You didn't need to do that you know. I feel bad. You're in my house; I should be a better host."

He sat down on the sofa beside her and put his arm around her shoulders. "Do you see me as your guest and you as the host?"

She shook her head with a smile.

"Me neither. You said it this morning and it made me happy. I want there to be an us, too. And if there is, then I'm going to pull my weight, not just mooch off you."

She laughed. "You're hardly mooching."

"I know, but you know what I mean. I want you to be my lady, and I want to take care of my lady. I guess, the way I grew up, there were very fixed gender roles. The men worked and the women took care of the house. I'm not looking for that." He felt dumb as he explained it. He should hardly be laying out how he saw a good marriage working—not when they'd only just started seeing each other.

Maria didn't seem to mind. "I grew up in that kind of community, too. And I'm sure as hell not looking to live that way. So, thank you." She laughed. "I suppose we should just get it straight up front. I don't mind doing for you—just don't come to expect it."

He laughed with her. "Fair enough. As long as you remember that I don't mind doing for you and you can expect it."

"Aww." She rested her head against his shoulder and looked up into his eyes in the way that made his heart feel like it was melting. "You're so sweet. You look like a big grouchy macho man, but when you scratch the surface, you're all soft underneath."

He rolled his eyes. "If you say so."

Her eyes twinkled, she loved teasing him. "I say so. All soft and sweet."

He narrowed his eyes and took hold of her hand, bringing it rest on his crotch. "Not *all* soft." Just the feel of her hand covering him had him rock hard again.

Her eyes widened in surprise. "I thought he'd be worn out after today."

Zack chuckled. "So did I, but he needs to prove to you that he's not soft."

"Well, I'd better take him to bed and see what he has to tell me."

Zack frowned. He hadn't thought this out. Of course, he wanted to take her to bed again, but they needed to talk about what they were going to do—tonight and tomorrow.

Her smile faded. "You don't want to?"

"You know I do, but let's talk about it first. If we want to keep what we're doing a secret, then I don't think my truck should be parked outside your house all night, do you?"

"Oh! No, of course not."

"And what time do you have to go to work in the morning?"

"I usually leave here around nine, but I can go later. The store doesn't open until ten."

He nodded. "And what time do you finish?"

"Six."

"How would you feel about your car breaking down?"

She frowned. "I'd be screwed."

He couldn't help it. He landed a kiss on her lips. "That's what I'm aiming for. What I mean about your car, though, is that if it's out of action then you're going to need a ride to work and home again, until it's fixed, right?"

A smile spread across her face as she understood what he was getting at. "Yes, please."

"Okay, so your car just broke down. That will give me an excuse to spend time with you every morning and every evening this week, and since we're doing that, it wouldn't be unreasonable for us to maybe have a dinner together one night—since we're such good friends." He smiled. "Maybe you're buying me dinner to say thank you for all the rides."

She nodded. "That sounds like something I would do."

"But it doesn't help us out tonight."

"You're right. Your truck has been outside all day. I didn't even think about that. But I don't want you to go. I want you to stay with me, or I'll stay with you."

Zack thought about it. "You need to get ready for work in the morning."

She shrugged. "I can bring what I need with me and get ready at your place."

He smiled, glad that she was looking for solutions rather than problems. "Always the positive peanut, right?"

She slapped his arm with a laugh. "I don't think I like that."

He held his hands up. "I mean it in the nicest possible way. It's supposed to be a compliment."

She pursed her lips. "Okay. I might let you off, as long as you figure out how we get to spend the night together." She stopped and looked up at him. "Does that make me sound terrible?"

"No. It makes me happy that you want to—and that you're comfortable enough to say so."

She relaxed. "That's right. That's what it is. It's just because I'm so comfortable with you. I wouldn't be like this with some other guy. I don't want you to think that."

Zack clenched his jaw. He didn't want to think of her with some other guy at all, let alone think about how willing and eager she might be to spend the night with him. "I don't. We've been friends for long enough that we don't need to be coy. I want to spend the night with you, you want to spend it with me. All we need to do is figure out how to make it happen without anyone knowing about it."

"Well, the way I see it, I could come with you in your truck and stay at your place."

"Or, I could take my truck home and walk back here. So that it looks like I'm home."

Maria smiled. "And maybe leave a landing light on to make it look like you're there?"

"I could." He was glad she was getting into the idea of what they needed to do. Even though she seemed to be treating it as a game, at least she was going along with it. "I think I'll do that. I'll take the truck now and then come straight back."

"I'll leave the backdoor unlocked so you can some straight in."

"That's a good idea. I'll just come around there and let myself in."

She nodded happily. "Maybe I'll be waiting in the kitchen for a repeat performance."

He raised an eyebrow at her and smiled. "Maybe I want to take you upstairs for something new and different?"

Her eyes widened. "Ooh! I'm in, either way."

Chapter Nine

Maria looked over at Zack as he pulled the truck out of her driveway the next morning. "Thank you."

He smiled at her. "What for?"

She shrugged. "For staying with me last night. For finally opening up to me. For everything."

"I'm the one who should be thanking you. For being so understanding about the situation I'm in, for still being open to this after I treated you as just a friend for all this time. Especially, for not meeting someone else while I was hiding how I felt. Every time I fly back in here, I'm scared that I'm going to hear that you started seeing someone."

She reached across and took hold of his hand. "There was no danger of that happening. I was too busy crushing on you. And since I'm such a positive peanut, I never stopped hoping that one day something might happen between us."

He squeezed her hand. "I'm glad you had enough faith for both of us. I spent half the time telling myself that nothing could happen and the other half hoping that you wouldn't meet someone else."

"Well, all that's behind us now. Now, we get to find out what's ahead of us."

His brows came down and for a moment, she panicked. Was he thinking that there wasn't anything ahead of them? That they'd already done what he wanted—slept together—and that was it? No. She forced herself to breathe deeply. That was a stupid idea and she knew it. He didn't just want to sleep with her. He liked her, he cared about her. He'd already said plenty of things that indicated he wanted them to have a real relationship.

Instead of letting herself get carried away worrying, it was better to just ask him. "Why does that bother you?"

He glanced over at her. "Because I dread what might be ahead of us. I won't be able to relax and really look forward to the future until ..." He shook his head. "I still don't think I should tell you about it."

She nodded. "That's up to you. I trust your judgment. But once that's all taken care of ..." She stopped herself before she asked the question that might seem like she was getting ahead of herself.

He smiled and answered it anyway. "Yes. I do want to see what's ahead for us. I'm very hopeful about what's ahead for us—and I'd like it to last a very, very long time."

Her heart raced happily. She would too.

She looked out the window when Zack came to a halt at the red light on the end of Main Street. The guy in the truck beside them turned at the same time and grinned. It was Logan. He rolled his window down and gestured for her to do the same.

"Morning guys! You two are out and about early." He raised his eyebrows. "Or are you on the way home?"

Maria laughed. "We're not all alley cats like you, Logan. Zack's a gentleman. He's giving me a ride to work because my car broke down."

Logan cocked his head to one side. "I can take you. I'm on my way over to Four Mile." He leaned forward to look past her at Zack. "There's no need to go all that way out of your way, bro." He grinned at Maria. "I'll be happy to give her a ride."

Maria's heart raced. She could feel Zack's agitation beside her. There was no way she was getting out of his truck to get in with Logan—even though it was nice of him to offer and would make much more sense. She turned to look at Zack. He leaned forward to smile at Logan. "Thanks bud, I wish I'd known you were going over there, but I said I'd stop in and see Roxy while I'm there anyway."

Logan shrugged. "Okay. But remember you can't hog all the hot chicks." He winked at Maria. "Next time you want a ride you come see me."

She rolled her eyes at him. "Not going to happen, Logan." She was glad when the light changed, and Zack pulled away. He pressed the button and the window rolled back up.

"That's all we need." Zack looked irritated.

"It's not a problem. I don't know why he's going in so late today, but he's usually over there by seven and doesn't leave till late."

She smiled to herself as she noticed his jaw clench tight.

"The only reason I know that is because he was giving Angel a ride every morning when her arm was in a cast. I don't pay attention to his comings and goings as a matter of course."

He smiled through pursed lips. "I really am a jealous asshole, aren't I?"

"Not an asshole, no. But don't go getting jealous, okay? If I wanted to see someone else, I would have. I've told you before, I only had eyes for the tall, dark, handsome mystery man who kept me in the friend zone."

He smiled and reached over to rest his hand on her thigh. "You're not in the friend zone anymore."

She laughed. "I know. I'm now firmly in the fuck zone."

To her surprise, he didn't laugh with her. "No. That makes it sound cheap. That's not what you are to me. You're more than that, much more than that."

She'd only been joking and was surprised by how seriously he'd taken it. "What zone am I in now, then?" she asked, trying to lighten things back up.

"You're in the girlfriend zone—if you want to be."

That put the smile back on her face. "I want to be."

~ ~ ~

Zack couldn't believe how quickly the week flew by. Usually, his time off here in Summer Lake dragged a little. Not this week. He and Maria quickly fell into an easy routine. He spent his nights at her place. And in the morning, he ran back to his house to get his truck and drove over to pick her up. In the evenings he went to the store in the plaza at Four Mile to collect her and bring her home. On Monday he'd pretended to drop her off then gone and left his truck at home and walked back to her place. And that had become the routine.

Now it was Thursday. The week was almost over. He'd dropped her off at work this morning and brought himself to the Boathouse for a late breakfast.

He smiled when he saw Adam, Clay's security guy, sitting at the bar sipping a coffee.

"Morning."

"Hey, Adam. How's it going?"

Adam smiled. "It's going well. Has Clay told you about the change of plans yet?"

"No." Zack's heart sank. He loved his job flying for Clay, and up until this week, he'd enjoyed the uncertainty of it. There was always a chance that Clay would call in the morning and say he needed to go somewhere that day. It had suited Zack well to not have a fixed schedule or location. Now he could only hope that Clay hadn't decided he needed to go back to Nashville today instead of on Monday.

Adam grinned. "Don't look like that. He's decided he'd going to stay another couple of weeks. You'll still have to go to Nashville on Monday, but it'll just be a quick turnaround. You'll be picking Autumn up and bringing her back here."

Zack smiled. "Okay."

Adam cocked his head to one side. "Does that suit you? I never know with you. I know Luke wants to spend as much time as he can here because of Angel, but you don't have anyone here. I thought maybe you'd be happier in Nashville. There's more to do—more opportunities."

Zack bristled at his statement that he didn't have anyone here. His first instinct was to set him straight and tell him that he did have someone, but he forced himself to bite it back. It was good that Adam had no clue. "I enjoy spending time here. I have good friends here."

Adam nodded and gave him a puzzled look. "Is there a girl?"

It chafed to have to say no. He didn't like to lie, but more than that, he didn't want to deny that he was with Maria. He wanted the whole world to know that somehow, he'd gotten lucky enough that the curvy, upbeat, beautiful Maria was interested in him. That she was sleeping with him every night, and that she was happy for him to call her his girlfriend—even if he couldn't say it in public. He shook his head.

Adam gave him a rueful smile. "I know the feeling. With jobs like ours, it's difficult, right?"

"Right."

He turned when the door opened, and two girls came in. They both had shoulder- length hair—one blonde, one brunette—but despite their different coloring, it was obvious they were sisters.

"Nice."

He turned to look at Adam and raised an eyebrow.

"I meant for you, not for me. They're a bit young for me, but just when you were lamenting that you don't have a girl, those two walk in. You should go say hi ... it might be fate."

Zack shook his head. "Nah. I'm not interested. I'm just here to eat." He made his way to a corner booth and picked up the menu.

The girls sat down just across from him. They were attractive, he could see that, but they did nothing for him. He only had eyes for a short, curvy, dark-haired beauty, who ... he checked his watch ... he'd be able to see again in another seven hours.

He watched as Austin came in through the doors and looked around. He smiled when he spotted the girls and came straight to them.

"Hi, ladies. What's the news on Lenny?"

"She's doing well, thanks. I've just come back from the hospital. She's eager to get home and said she'd rather I was here getting things ready than sitting around there staring at her."

Austin chuckled. "That's good. It sounds like she's getting back to normal."

Zack watched Austin curiously. These were obviously Lenny's granddaughters who Logan had been teasing him about at the weekend. He'd thought it was probably just Logan joking around as he did but seeing the way Austin's ears had turned red and the way he shifted from one foot to the other whenever the blonde sister looked at him, there might be something in it.

"She is doing much better, but I want her to stay at home for a while. She's talking about getting straight back to work, and we can't let her do that," said the blonde.

"No. She's going to need to rest up for a while," agreed Austin. "Is she going to come and stay at the house with you?"

"That's what we'd hoped," said the darker haired of the two, "but she insists she wants to go home. "I guess we'll have to take turns to stay with her and work the post office."

"Well, there are plenty of folks in town who'll be happy to pitch in and lend a hand. Your grandmother is well-liked and respected. Don't hesitate to ask if you need any help, will you?"

They both smiled at him.

Zack felt bad for eavesdropping, but he was curious whether Austin was here on business or just to check in with the girls. He knew Nadia would not be pleased if it were the latter. He coughed. It was only fair to let Austin know that he was there.

Austin turned and looked guilty as hell when he saw Zack. He recovered quickly, but not before he'd confirmed Zack's suspicion that he was interested in the fairer sister.

"Oh. Hey, Zack. I didn't see you there." Austin smiled. "I should introduce you. This is Zack Aguila, he's a friend and part-time Summer Lake resident. Zack, this is Amber and Jade Kerrigan. They're Lenny's granddaughters."

Zack smiled at them. "Nice to meet you ladies. I hope your grandma is feeling better?"

"She is, thank you. We're expecting to get her home tomorrow," the blonde, whom he now knew was Amber, gave him a friendly smile.

Jade arched an eyebrow at him. "How come you're only a part-time resident here?"

Zack stared at her for a moment, a little taken aback by such a forthright question. He wasn't used to answering direct questions about himself. He was a private person by nature, not just because his circumstances required it. Added to that, he didn't like to advertise that he flew for Clay McAdam. He respected Clay's right to privacy as much as his own.

Austin chuckled to cover the awkward silence that was developing. "Zack's a pilot. He graces us with his presence every so often."

Zack smiled and nodded and looked up gratefully as the server hurried toward him brandishing a coffee-pot. "Hi, sorry to keep you waiting. Do you want a coffee to get you started?"

"That'd be great, thanks." He smiled at Austin and the girls. "It was nice to meet you," he told them and then returned his attention to studying the menu. Hoping they'd take the hint that as far as he was concerned, the conversation was over. Austin might be happy to chat with them and not be concerned about what his girlfriend might think, but Zack had no interest in any female other than the one he couldn't even say was his girlfriend.

He was relieved to see Luke walk in. He hadn't talked to him much this week. He raised a hand when Luke looked around, then he thought better of it and got to his feet, taking his coffee and his menu with him. He'd rather go and sit somewhere else where he and Luke could catch up and talk freely without those girls—especially the dark-haired one being able to listen in.

"Hey, bro. What are you doing here?" asked Luke.

"I could ask you the same thing."

Luke shrugged. "I'm going out of my mind. I've done everything I can think of at the house—I even cleaned behind the fridge."

Zack laughed. "Damn, it must be bad."

Luke nodded. "I love being back here, but it sucks being at a loose end all day while Angel's working and only getting to see her in the evening."

"Tell me about it." Zack wished he could take the words back as soon as they were out.

Luke gave him a puzzled look. "Are you going to eat? Do you want to grab a booth and you can tell me what you mean by that? Though I think I can probably guess."

Zack nodded and led him to a booth on the other side of the restaurant.

"So?" asked Luke. "Am I right in guessing that you're getting bored sitting around waiting for Maria to get off work?"

He nodded.

Luke smiled at him. "And do I have a sneaky, suspicious mind, or is there nothing wrong with her car really?"

Zack's heart sank. He'd been hoping that was a plausible enough reason for him to be giving Maria a ride to and from work every day. "You are one of the least sneaky and suspicious people I know. So, I guess it wasn't a very good cover story."

Luke grinned. "No. I don't think anyone else would give it a second thought. It's only because I know. If you hadn't told me when we were in here on Saturday that you'd finally crumbled and spent the afternoon with her, then I don't think I would have blinked about it. It just sounded a little too coincidental, given the timing."

"Yeah. I suppose."

Luke gave him a reassuring smile. "I don't think anyone thought Angel was carrying on with Logan when he was giving her a ride to work every day."

"True, but then her arm was in a cast and she couldn't drive herself." He shook his head. "You don't think he likes Maria, do you?"

Luke laughed. "I hate to break it to you, but she has breasts, so yeah, of course Logan likes her. He likes anything with breasts and a pulse."

Zack had to laugh. "You've got a point there. I guess I'm getting a bit territorial."

"Well, I don't think you've got any worries. I got Angel talking about it, and she said that Maria's liked you since the first time she met you—and she hasn't dated anyone else since then."

Zack smiled. "I know ... she told me that herself."

"So, is this serious—or going somewhere serious?"

"I'd like to think so."

"But you're going to keep it hidden?"

Zack nodded.

"Because you don't want some shadowy figure from your mysterious past to find out about Maria?"

He nodded again.

"And what? What do you think would happen? Do you seriously think that someone would hurt her or kidnap her ... or what? Sorry. I don't know what I'm talking about, and to be honest, I'm finding it hard to even imagine it. I mean, shit like that doesn't happen in real life."

"Maybe not in your life." Zack was on the verge of telling him the whole thing. He was tired of hiding. Tired of hiding in the hopes of never being found and tired of hiding his past from his friends—especially Luke who had been such a good friend.

"Are you ready to order?" The server appeared beside them and Zack nodded. It was probably for the best. Even if he was ready to tell Luke, he should do it somewhere more private than this where anyone could overhear them.

Luke gave him a rueful smile once she'd gone. "You're getting closer to filling me in, aren't you?"

"I am."

"Maybe when we go back to Nashville on Monday?"

"Oh, haven't you heard?"

Luke shook his head.

"I saw Adam when I came in. He told me that Clay had a change of plans. He's staying here. We still need to go, but only to collect Autumn and bring her back."

Luke grinned. "That's awesome. Do you know how long he wants to stay?"

"A couple of weeks, Adam said."

"I need to tell Angel."

Zack envied his friend as he watched him tap out a text to let Angel know he was going to be around for a while longer. He wanted to tell Maria, but they'd agreed that they should keep their phone calls and texts to a minimum—just in case.

Chapter Ten

"Do you want to do the safe or the cash register tonight?" asked Laura.

"I'll do the safe," answered Maria and went to lock the front door and flip the sign over to tell the world they were closed. She paused when she noticed someone lurking in the doorway of the beauty salon across the way. Goose bumps ran down her arms as the man turned and looked at her and then moved farther inside, out of sight.

She shook her head and turned back to start collecting the trays from the display cases. She was being silly. It was probably some poor husband waiting for his wife to come out. She took the first set of trays into the back and started loading up the safe for the night.

"Is Zack coming for you tonight?" asked Laura.

Maria bit back a smile. She hoped so; in fact, she planned to make sure he did. "He is."

Laura gave her an inquiring look. "It's good of him to bring you and collect you every day like this. How long do you think it's going to take for your car to be fixed?"

"They're going to work on it this weekend. I should have it back by Monday." She hated lying. It was safe to say that she'd be using her own car again by Monday, since that was the day Zack was going back to Nashville.

Laura nodded thoughtfully. "You should give him a shot."

Maria looked up in surprise. "What … what do you mean?"

Laura smiled. "I know he's a good guy and everything, but do you really think he's going all this way out of his way—twice a day just because he's a nice guy? I think he's interested in you."

Maria shrugged. She didn't know what to say. She'd love to tell Laura that yes, he was interested in her—and she was interested in him.

"Don't tell me you don't like him. I remember the first time he came in here with Smoke. I thought the two of you were a sure thing."

Maria shrugged. "Of course, I like him. Come on, he's gorgeous!"

Laura chuckled. "I'm not saying anything—so you won't hear me disagree with you."

Maria laughed. "I'm sure you don't notice other good-looking guys. I mean why would you? You've got Smoke."

Laura waggled her eyebrows. "I notice—I'm a jeweler, I admire things of beauty. But I'm not interested, and I don't feel the need to comment."

"Is that because Smoke wouldn't like it? He's a bit on the possessive side, isn't he?"

Laura laughed. "Just a teeny bit. I always thought I couldn't stand a guy who was jealous or possessive, but it's just a part of who Smoke is. I understand why he acts that way—it stems from his past. And he's not over the top with it, he's just honest. And besides," she shrugged, "I kind of like it. He never leaves me in any doubt about the fact that he loves me and wants me to be all his."

Maria smiled at her. That was how Zack was, too. Except she didn't know enough about his past to know if that was why he was like that.

"It strikes me that Zack and Smoke are quite similar."

Maria nodded. "Maybe."

Laura held her gaze for a long moment. "Are you hiding something?"

Maria stared back into her eyes. How could she lie?

"You are, aren't you?" Laura grinned. "I knew it! He's not just giving you a ride to work and back, is he?"

"I can't say anything."

"You don't need to. It's written all over your face. Right now, you look guilty as hell, and all week you've been starry-eyed. What's the big secret?"

"I'm not admitting anything, but you know Zack is a very private person."

Laura frowned. "Are you telling me that you're sleeping with him, and he doesn't want anyone to know about it?"

"It's not like that."

Laura folded her arms across her chest. "What is it like then? Tell me you're not just his booty call? You're worth so much more than that."

Maria smiled. "No. It's really not like that. I want to tell you, but we're supposed to be keeping it a secret."

"Why?! Tell me he's not hiding something?"

"He is, he's hiding the fact that that he cares about me, to keep me safe."

Laura looked skeptical. "Safe from what?"

They both turned at the sound of a knock on the back door. "Hey, lady. It's me," Smoke's voice called. "Can I come in? I found a Zack lurking out here, too."

Maria gave Laura a pleading look and spoke in a low voice. "Please don't call him out on it. It's not like you think. He cares about me. That's why he's doing it. He's not just using me, I promise you."

Laura made a face at her and went to open the back door.

Smoke came in and kissed her cheek. "I got finished early. I thought you might want to have a drink at the Lodge before we go home."

Laura smiled at him. "That sounds great." She turned to Zack. "And you're here playing taxi for Maria again?"

Zack smiled at her. "I sure am."

Laura gave him a long, appraising look, and Maria was sure she was going to say something. She let out the breath she didn't know she'd been holding when Laura nodded. "It's good of you to step in and help."

Zack nodded. "That's what friends are for."

Laura looked at Maria. "Why don't you get going. You don't want to keep your friend waiting."

Maria didn't like to leave before everything was finished up, but she was glad to get out of here before Laura decided to start interrogating Zack. It was obvious that she thought he was just using her for sex. It was also obvious that she didn't like that idea and wanted to protect Maria. "Okay, if you're sure."

Laura nodded. "Yeah. Go on. I leave you to close up by yourself more often than not."

Smoke smiled at her when she picked up her purse. "I hope you're going to buy him dinner to say thank you for chauffeuring you around all week."

Maria nodded.

"She doesn't need to do that," said Zack.

Laura scowled at him. "I'm sure she's already thanked you enough."

Maria scurried for the door. This was getting awkward and she just wanted to leave. "See you tomorrow," she said with a smile and hurried out.

Zack followed and caught up to her at his truck. "What was all that about?"

Maria made a face. "I'll tell you on the way home." She wanted to kiss him when he got into the driver's seat and turned to smile at her, but she didn't dare.

He started the engine and backed out. "What's going on?" he asked as he pulled away from the plaza and out onto the main road heading back to town.

She blew out a sigh. "Laura was suggesting that maybe you had an ulterior motive for driving me around all week."

Zack smiled. "I do."

"Yes, but I kind of messed up. I couldn't keep the secret very well. She was saying I should give you a chance, and I didn't say anything, but she picked up on the fact that I already had. She's got it in her head that you want to sleep with me, but that you don't want anyone to know about it." She sighed. "Which is kind of true, but not for the reasons that she thinks."

Zack frowned. "She thinks I'm just using you as a booty call?"

Maria nodded.

"But why would I want to keep that secret?"

Maria shrugged. "Maybe she thinks you're ashamed of me."

"Why?! Why would she say that?"

"She didn't; maybe that's just me."

"You don't seriously think I'm ashamed of you, do you?"

"No. I don't. I know why you want to keep us a secret. Well, I kind of do."

"It's to keep you off the radar. So, that if the people who are looking for me find me, they won't have any reason to come after you as well. That's all it is, Maria."

"I know. I understand that. It was just that for a moment there, when Laura thought you were keeping me as your dirty little secret, I started to think that maybe she was right."

"Well, she's not. She couldn't be more wrong. You're not a dirty little secret. You're the hardest secret I've ever had to keep. I want to tell the world that you're my girl, that I'm the lucky bastard who gets to be with you. I want to tell every other guy that you're taken, you're mine."

She gave him a small smile. "You mean that, don't you?"

"More than you know."

"Maybe one day we'll be able to."

"We will. And I'm going to do what I can to make sure that day comes sooner rather than later."

"What do you mean?"

"I mean, I'm tired of hiding. I don't want to keep what's going on between us a secret. I want to start thinking about us having a future, and I can't do that until I deal with my past."

Maria's heart started to race. "What are you going to do?"

"I don't know. I'm going to start by talking to my dad."

Maria's eyes widened. "Do you realize that's the first time you've mentioned your family?"

"I do. One day soon, you'll understand why. But I'll talk to him this weekend. I'll tell him about you. Well, he already knows about you. He's known since we first met, but now he needs to know that I failed."

"Failed? At what."

He glanced over at her, his expression unreadable. "Do you remember our first dance?"

Maria nodded. She'd gone over that night so many times. She'd thought it was going to be the night they got together; but instead, it was the night that he'd distanced himself from her.

"I'd talked to my dad before I came out that night. I told him about you, I told him I was going to ask you out, and he warned me that I shouldn't. He told me I had to hide my heart from you to keep you safe. Now I have to tell him that my heart refuses to hide anymore so we need to come up with a new plan."

Maria sat back in her seat. If she was honest, she'd had an inkling that Zack might be hiding her from his family. He never talked about them. Though he didn't hide the fact that he came from money. She'd thought that maybe they wouldn't approve of her, that they might think she wasn't good enough for him.

He glanced over at her and she gave him a weak smile. "I don't know what to say."

"Just tell me if you think I'm worth it."

She laughed. "Of course you are."

"Good. Then I'm going to find a way for us to be together and not have to hide it from anyone."

Instead of going to Maria's, Zack carried on past her road and went to his house. It bothered him that she had doubts about his intentions. To be fair, they were Laura's doubts, but he needed Maria to understand how important she was to him. If she was thinking that maybe he saw her as a friend with benefits, he needed to show her that she meant so much more than that to him. It wouldn't be easy to show her while keeping their relationship a secret, but he figured he'd have a better chance in his own house than by spending all their time at her place.

He pulled the truck into the garage and waited until the door rolled down behind them.

She turned and smiled at him. "Did you come to get something, or are we staying here?"

He smiled. "I thought we could stay here tonight. I can cook for you."

"Ooh. I like the sound of that. What are we having?"

"Pasta. I'm not the world's greatest chef, but I make a mean spaghetti, and you haven't tried it yet."

He climbed out of the truck and waited for her at the door that led into the house. Once they were inside, he locked the door behind them and pressed her up against it. "I missed you today. I miss you every day."

She looped her arms up around his neck and landed a kiss on his lips. "I missed you, too. And I'm going to miss you even more next week."

"You won't get a chance to. Clay changed his mind. He's staying here for a few weeks. Do you think you can stand to have me around for longer?"

She rubbed herself against him. "I think I can stand it. As long as you're going to take care of me." She made her meaning apparent when she took his hands and placed them on her ass.

"Take care of you? Is that what we're calling it now?" He backed her against the door and pressed his hard-on between her legs.

She nodded breathlessly. "I don't see why not."

"Do you want me to take care of you right now?" He dropped his head and spoke the words into the soft skin of her neck, making her shudder, which in turn made him harder for her.

"Right now," she breathed, and began to fumble with the zipper on his jeans before pushing them and his boxers down over his hips.

It seemed she was in a hurry and he was happy to oblige. There was no time to go upstairs or even as far as the sofa in the living room. He pushed her skirt up around her waist and slid his fingers inside her panties. She was already soaking. He couldn't resist thrusting his finger deep, loving the needy little moan that escaped from her lips.

Her sense of urgency had affected him, though. This wasn't the time for finesse.

"Give it to me, Zack," she murmured. "Give it to me hard."

She didn't need to say another word.

He hooked his arm behind her leg and brought it up to wrap around his, spreading her wide open. His cock throbbed when it found her wet heat, but before he had a chance to slide inside, she thrust her hips and impaled herself on him with a low moan of, "Fuck me, Zack."

His hips obeyed her command without a conscious thought from him. He clamped her leg to his side and drove deep and hard, over and over, showing her no mercy as she clung to him, gasping out her pleasure. He lost himself inside her every time. She was so wet, so tight, clenching around him and promising to take everything he had to give.

He didn't last long before he gave it to her. Her low moans and gasps built to a crescendo, and when she screamed his name, he let go, finding his release deep inside her. He came hard as she gripped him tight, pulsating around him as wave after wave of pleasure carried them away.

When they finally stilled, she looked up into his eyes. "Told you I missed you."

He chuckled. "I told you I missed you, too."

She smiled. "If we can only just make it inside the house after not seeing each other all day, what are we going to be like when we don't see each other for weeks?"

He shook his head. He'd been trying not to think about that. He already hated the thought of having to leave her. They both knew it would happen. He spent a lot of time here at the lake, but his job could take him anywhere at any time. "I think we should plan to get ahead of ourselves."

She gave him a puzzled look.

"Well, if we can only just manage to go eight hours before I have to make love to you again, then we should figure out how many multiples of hours we're going to be apart and try to get all our loving in before I go."

She laughed. "I like that idea, and we'd definitely be talking about multiples."

He landed a kiss on her soft sweet lips. "I think we should talk about those after dinner. I have a few ideas."

"Ooh. I'd love to hear about them."

He winked at her. "I'll be happy to show you."

~ ~ ~

Maria looked out the window when she heard a truck pull up outside. It wasn't Zack; it must be someone going to the neighbor's. She sighed and went back to the ironing board. It was Sunday afternoon. She'd spent the last few nights with Zack at his place, but this afternoon she'd told him that she needed to get her things ready for the week ahead. Sunday afternoon was ironing time, and as much as she'd rather spend it with him, she knew he had things to catch up on too. He had to talk to Luke and do their flight planning for their trip back to Nashville. And she hoped he'd call his father as well. He hadn't mentioned it again since the other night, but she was hoping that maybe if he talked to him, his dad might be able to help him.

She smiled as she picked up the iron again. She loved that his dad had known since the beginning that Zack cared about her. He must have known that his son's heart was involved for him to say that he should keep it hidden. She started ironing. She just hoped his dad would approve of her when he met her. She also hoped that her family would approve of Zack. But she didn't need to worry about that yet. She knew they wouldn't approve of them hiding their relationship. But they wouldn't even know about it until they didn't have to hide any more.

She jumped when she heard a crash in the back yard and went running to see what it was. She had to laugh when she got to the backdoor and realized that she'd unconsciously unplugged the iron and brought it with her. What did she plan to do, she wondered? Beat a burglar about the head with it? She set the iron down and opened the door.

The trash can was lying on its side but there was no one out there. She stood it back up and put a rock on the lid. She hoped there wasn't a rabid raccoon around—it was unusual for them to be out before dark.

Chapter Eleven

"What's your plan for this week?" asked Luke.

"What do you mean?"

"Well, last week Maria's car was supposedly broken down, so you gave her a ride to work and back. I'm assuming her car is miraculously fixed today and she's driving herself while we're here."

Zack nodded. "Yeah. I'm just going to have to wave her off in the morning and wait for her to get home. I liked driving her. It gave me an excuse to be outside her house twice a day. Now, I'll just have to be more careful."

"I understand a whole lot better now that you've explained it to me. I even understand why you didn't want to tell me. The fewer people who know the better, right? The less risk there is of someone inadvertently giving you away."

"Yup." They were sitting at the general aviation building at the airport in Nashville, waiting for Autumn who had some last-minute emergency and was running late.

Luke shook his head. "I can see why you'd want to turn the tables and hunt him down. Put an end to it on your terms before he finds you."

"Thanks. I'm hoping my dad will see it that way, too. In the beginning we had faith that they'd find him and put him behind bars, but since they haven't been able to ..." He shrugged. "It's time for me to be able to get on with my life without constantly looking over my shoulder."

"If there's anything I can do to help ... you know I'm in."

"Thanks, bro. I don't know what I can do myself yet, but if something comes up, it's good to know I've got you in my corner."

Luke smiled. "Always."

Zack's phone rang and he pulled it out of his pocket. "I need to take this. It's my dad. I'm going to take a walk around the parking lot. Come find me if Autumn shows up?"

"Sure thing."

Zack swiped to answer as he headed for the door. "Hey, Papá. What's up?"

"The FBI have a lead on him."

"They do? Where?"

"He was seen in Sacramento last week. It makes me nervous, Zack. That's too close. I think it's time for you to move on."

"No. I'm not moving on. I'm staying put this time."

The line was quiet for a long time. "The girl?"

"Yes. I did my best, but just a couple of weeks ago, I caved. We're together."

"You really want to put her in danger?"

"You know I don't. But I want to be with her. I was going to call you. I'm not going to run anymore, and I'm not going to hide. I couldn't hide my heart like you told me to."

He could hear the smile in his dad's voice. "I'm surprised you lasted as long as you did. When I told you that, I thought you'd find that either you couldn't do it or you'd lose interest."

"I did it for as long as I could, but I never lost interest. I'm being careful; we're hiding our relationship, but that can't last. I can't just wait for him to find me. I think it's time for me to find him."

"It's too dangerous, Zack."

"I have to do it. I can't live my life like this anymore. I want to be with Maria. I want the world to know that we're together. I want you to be able to come visit us. I want to bring her to meet you. I can't do any of that until this is over."

"And what do you plan to do?"

"I haven't gotten that far yet. The first thing I need to do is find him. That's going to be a whole lot easier now that I know he's in the country."

"If you're sure I can't talk you out of this, then I'd say it'd be easier to let him find you."

"That's true."

"But I don't think your Maria should be anywhere near you when he does."

"She doesn't know the whole story."

"Then maybe it's time you tell her and ask her if she wants to come here. She can stay with Carmen and me."

"I don't think she'd go for that. Her life is here, and her family is in Texas."

"I think she'd be safest here. So would you, if you'd come."

"Papá, I would have been safest with you for the last ten years. But you know I couldn't do that. I'd rather he found me and killed me. At least that way I'd die living. Staying with you might keep me alive longer, but I'd be dead inside, living a half-life."

"I know, *mi hijo*. But as your father, you know that a part of me would rather see you live a safe half-life, than worry every

morning when I wake up whether today will be the day that I
get the call that he found you."

"I know it's hard for you, and I love you for all the help
you've given me. But it's time to end it, one way or another."

"Well, if you're going to do this, you should talk to Manny
Alvarado, he's the special agent in charge of the Sacramento
field office now. Whether you plan to track Morales down or
use yourself as bait, he'll want to know what you're doing—
and he should be able to help."

"Thanks. I'll give him a call when I get back to the lake."

"Where are you now?"

"In Nashville, but it's only a quick turnaround. I'll be home
tonight."

"This scares me, Zack. But hearing you say that reassures me
that it's time."

"Say what?"

"You said when you're *home* tonight. You haven't called any
place home since Medellín."

Zack's heart raced. He hadn't noticed it, but now his dad
mentioned it, he knew it was true. "If this all works out, home
will be wherever she is."

"I gathered that much. I look forward to meeting her."

Maria finally gave in and made herself some dinner. She'd
wanted to wait for Zack to get back, but he'd texted her a little
while ago to say that they still weren't back in the air and he
didn't know what time he'd be home. They'd taken off later
than expected and then had to make a stop they hadn't been
planning on when Autumn had offered to drop Shawnee
Reynolds off in Phoenix.

She poured herself a soda and took her sad looking little dinner through to the living room. She knew she'd have to get used to this. And really, she was lucky he was coming back at all. They'd originally thought that when he went back to Nashville today, he'd be there for a couple of weeks.

Her phone rang just as she was finishing her sandwich and she grabbed for it. It wasn't Zack; it was Angel.

"Hey, girlfriend. How are you?"

"I'm good. I just got home from work and it turns out I could have stayed later. Luke just called to say that it's going to be at least another hour before they can take off again."

Maria sighed. She'd wished Zack could call her, but that was one of the downsides of them being a secret.

"Anyway, I'm trying to take a leaf out of your book and make the best of the time I now have free. So, I thought I'd call you and catch up. Do you want to have a girls' dinner on Thursday night? Roxy's off, so she can join us, and I'm sure Kenzie will be up for it. I thought we might invite Lenny's granddaughters—or at least one of them if one has to stay home with her. It sounds as though they plan to stay now that they're here, so I thought we should try to make them welcome."

"Yeah. That's a lovely idea."

"But what? You don't sound too enthused."

"Sorry. I am. We haven't had one of our dinners for a while, and it'd be nice to get to know Amber and Jade and make them feel welcome."

"But you'd rather stay in with Zack?"

Maria pursed her lips. She deliberately hadn't called Angel last week—since she knew she wouldn't be able to lie to her. "That's supposed to be a secret."

"Oh! I see. What, is it part of Zack's whole mystery man deal?"

"Yeah."

And you're not supposed to tell anyone that you're seeing each other?"

"No."

"Not even me?"

"I'm going to have a word with him about that. It's driving me nuts. I miss you. We talk all the time—about everything."

"I know. I've missed you, too. I guessed that you and Zack had gotten it together, and I was a bit surprised that you hadn't said anything, but I figured you would when you were ready."

"I've been dying to talk to you. But … well, to be fair. We've been spending all our time together anyway."

Angel chuckled. "I'm glad. Glad for the two of you, and glad that now you know how it is. You and Roxy tease me about spending all my time at work or with Luke, and now you know what it's like. It doesn't mean you don't want to see your friends … it's just that it all gets so busy and the time goes by before you know it."

"Yep. I apologize for ever giving you a hard time. I totally get it now."

"Well, how about we tell the girls we'll meet them for dinner at seven on Thursday and you and I can get together straight after work—that'll give us an hour to ourselves."

"Thanks, Angel. I'd like that."

Angel laughed. "And I'll suggest that Luke should take Zack out for dinner. I love having him back, but I didn't expect him to be here at all this week. One night apart won't kill us."

It was late when Zack brought the plane in to land at Summer Lake. Autumn apologized again for delaying them so much as they walked across the tarmac.

"It's not a problem," said Zack. "It's part of the job. We don't mind."

Autumn gave him a wry smile. "I know it's not a problem for you, but he," she jerked her head at Luke, "is no doubt in a hurry to get back to Angel."

Luke smiled. "I am, but then no matter how late we are tonight, I'm still coming back to her a couple of weeks earlier than I thought I'd be."

"That's true. I think I need to get used to the fact that I'm going to be spending more time here. Clay doesn't want to leave, and neither do you."

Zack wanted to add that he didn't want to leave either, but Autumn didn't need to know that, and neither did anyone else.

The flight school building stood in darkness, but headlights illuminated the parking lot. "That'll be Davin," said Autumn. "Clay said he'd be waiting for me."

Zack's heart raced, hoping she was right. Knowing that Morales was not only in the country but had been as close as Sacramento recently, had him on edge. He peered at the SUV as it pulled up to the gate, and relaxed a little when he saw Clay's second security guy, Davin, roll down the window.

"Evening guys."

"Hi Davin." Autumn opened the passenger door and turned back to smile at Zack and Luke. "Would you do me a favor and let me know if people are getting together to go out this week? I'm not thrilled at the thought of being cooped up in a cabin the whole time I'm here."

"Of course," said Luke. "I don't know what's happening in the week, but we usually all get together on the weekend, at least."

"Well, let me know."

Davin grinned at them over her shoulder. "I'd lay on a social life for her, if I were you guys. She's used to big city life. If you want to encourage her to keep coming here instead of making Clay go back to Nashville, you should find stuff for her to do."

Autumn laughed. "You know me too well, Davin. But I do like it here, and to be honest, I don't mind getting away from Nashville."

Davin gave her a stern look. "You know Matt can come out here just as easily as you can."

Autumn scowled at him. "Shut up, would you? Let's get going. You can buy me a drink at the bar before you drop me off."

Davin grinned at them before Autumn slammed the passenger door shut.

"Are you going to go to Maria's?" Luke asked as they walked to Zack's truck.

"Yeah. I'll drop you off, then I'll take the truck home and walk over to her place."

"Next time we fly, we should come in my truck, then I can drop you off at her place. We said we were going to take turns."

"Thanks. That's a good idea."

Maria turned the volume down on the TV when she heard a noise out back. It was most likely Zack, but she grabbed the rolling pin from the drawer on her way through the kitchen to investigate.

She instinctively started to raise it when the door handle turned, then tried to hide it behind her back when she saw Zack. He grinned at her and came in, locking the door behind him.

"Hey, beautiful. Sorry it got so late."

She went to him with a smile, setting the rolling pin down on the counter before she slipped her arms around his waist. "That's okay. I'm just glad you're back tonight."

He glanced at the rolling pin and gave her a puzzled look. "For a minute there I thought you were going to beat me for being so late."

She laughed. "No. I was going to beat anyone who wasn't you."

He frowned. "Are you edgy about something?"

She shrugged. "There was a raccoon out back this afternoon."

"There was?"

She pursed her lips. "At least. I assumed it was a raccoon. I heard a noise out there and came to investigate. The trash can had been knocked over and … oh … you don't think it was …" She shuddered at the thought that it might not have been a raccoon at all.

Zack looked worried. "Maybe it was, but I don't think we should be taking any chances."

"Why? Has something happened?"

He blew out a sigh. "Maybe not. But it's going to."

"What do you mean?"

"I talked to my dad. He told me that the guy—his names is Morales—was seen in Sacramento last week. That's too close for comfort."

A shiver ran down Maria's spine. She hadn't been able to take this mysterious threat too seriously. Up until now, it had been more like a story. Now, with the thought that someone might have been in her back yard this afternoon, it seemed a lot more real. "What do you think we should do?"

"I think I need to call the FBI field office in Sacramento. And I think we should spend the night at my place. At least I have an alarm system. Do you want to get some things together while I make the call?"

"Okay."

He held her close to his chest. "I'm sorry. I never wanted to put you in harm's way."

She looked up into his eyes. "I'm fine. What about you? If he's here, he's here for you."

"He is. And I'm ready for him. It's time to put an end to this."

"What does that mean, Zack? I don't even know who he is or why he's after you."

He pursed his lips. "You go get ready. I'll call Manny. I'll tell you more once we get out of here."

"Manny Alvarado."

"Manny. It's Zack Aguila."

"Has he showed up there?"

Zack blew out a sigh. "I don't know. Maybe not, but there was someone in my girlfriend's back yard this afternoon." He shook his head. "To be honest, that someone may have been a raccoon. But I spoke to my dad earlier and he said you had a lead on Morales there in Sacramento."

"We did. I'm glad you called."

"Let me guess. You were waiting to see if he was coming here?"

"We were. I didn't want to alert you. I wanted to see if we could catch up with him."

"Well, it looks like he's caught up with me."

"I'll have guys up there by morning. And I'll be with them."

"You don't know that it wasn't a raccoon yet."

"I think we both know he's coming, if he's not there already. And you have a girlfriend? Why didn't you tell me?"

"Because we've been keeping it quiet."

"I need to know that kind of thing, Zack."

"Well, you know now. And you should also know that I'm not going to run this time. You come up here. You help me put a stop to him if you can. But this is it. I'm standing my ground."

"Don't make any hasty decisions, Zack."

"After ten years, you can hardly say I'm being hasty. I'm done, Manny. I want to be able to get on with my life. I want to be able to take my girl out in public and have the world know that we're together."

Manny blew out a sigh. "I understand, but if that's what you want, we need you both alive for it to happen. Is the house secure?"

"Yeah, and we're heading back there now."

"Let me know when you're there. And tomorrow you stay there till we arrive."

"No. If he is here, you'll scare him off. I want to draw him out this time."

Manny sighed again. "We can talk about that tomorrow. You go home, you lock it down, and you wait for me to call you in the morning."

"Okay."

Zack hung up and turned to see Maria standing in the kitchen doorway. "This is all feels very real all of a sudden."

He went to her and closed his arms around her. "It is. How would you feel about staying home tomorrow?"

She smiled. "Not a problem. I was going to surprise you with that in the morning. Laura asked if I could switch my day off. So, I'm home tomorrow anyway."

"That's good. That'll give us time to figure out what we do from here."

She looked up at him. Her eyes were full of questions, but he didn't know where to start explaining. Instead, he lowered his lips to hers and kissed her deeply.

Chapter Twelve

Maria opened her eyes and lay there for a moment. She was already used to sleeping in Zack's bed with him. She loved it. She loved being close to him. Loved the way he slept with his arm over her middle, and sometimes in the night he drew her closer while he slept.

"Are you awake?"

She looked up at him. "Almost."

He smiled and landed a kiss on her lips. She knew her face was probably still puffy with sleep, but she didn't care. When she'd been with guys in the past, she hated them to see her in the morning. It wasn't like that with Zack. He proved her point by kissing one eyelid and then the other. "You're so cute when you wake up."

She laughed. "Yeah, cute like a rodent coming out of hibernation."

"No. Cute like my gorgeous woman waking up in my arms."

She shook her head at him. "Thanks. Flattery will get you everywhere with me, but then you already knew that. You don't look like you just woke up, though."

His smile faded. "No. I've been thinking."

She rolled on her stomach to look him in the eye. "What about?"

"About what's going to happen. We don't know that it was him in your back yard last night. It might have been nothing more than a raccoon. But even if he's not here. He's coming. I know he is. And Manny must believe it, too, or he wouldn't be on his way up here."

"Are you going to tell me the rest of the story yet?"

He nodded and sat up. She sat beside him, leaning back against the headboard and covering her breasts with the sheet.

He ran his hand over her and cupped one breast, teasing her nipple through the sheet. She closed her eyes and fought her need for him. It'd be too easy to allow him to distract her like that. "Not yet, Zack. I need to know."

"I'm sorry." He dropped his hand and closed it around hers. "I don't know where to start."

"The beginning is usually a good place."

He smiled. "I don't even know where that is." He turned to stare out the window for a moment and she waited, wondering what she was about to hear. "I think you already know that I come from money."

She nodded. "I don't know anything about you for certain, but yeah, it's kind of obvious that your family must be wealthy.

"Very. My dad owns a bank. Amongst other things. You know Eddie?"

"April's Eddie?"

"Yes. His dad, Ted, is my dad's partner."

"Wow. I would never have guessed that you two knew each other. I thought if anything maybe you knew April. You seem to be … I don't know … more familiar with her."

He gave her a half smile. "Not that kind of familiar."

She gave a guilty little laugh. "Okay, you got me. When I first knew you, and you made it clear that you weren't interested in me, it bothered me a little. It didn't seem fair that April—who was already engaged to the lovely Eddie, should also be the one girl in town who you were less stand-offish with."

He smiled and tucked a strand of hair behind her ear. "You were jealous?"

She shrugged. "Maybe a little. But you only know her because of Eddie?"

"Kind of. I spent some time in Montana. The bank foreclosed the loan on her ex-husband's property, and Ted wanted to make sure that it was all set up to be held in trust until her son Marcus comes of age. I went up there to oversee everything."

"Wow. I had no idea. Eddie must be really good at keeping secrets."

"He is, but then I don't know him that well. He and his dad were estranged for many years. It's not like I grew up knowing him. Besides, my dad was in charge of the South and Central American assets, which meant he spent most of his time overseas. I grew up in Colombia."

"Wow! I bet that was interesting. I've heard it's changed a lot in the last few years, but it used to be a pretty dangerous place, didn't it?"

"It did."

"Oh! Is that where this Morales person is from?"

He nodded. "Colombia used to be the kidnapping capital of the world. I was taken when I was twenty-two."

"Oh, my God, Zack! What happened?"

He pursed his lips. "I was just a kid. I'd been out with some friends. I was crossing the street, going back to my driver, who was also my bodyguard. Two cars pulled up, they bundled me inside and drove away. Simple as that. They held me in a basement for eleven weeks." He shook his head. "I tried to escape, and they beat me for it. My dad was beside himself. He promised to give them whatever they wanted. He told me to do whatever they said, and he'd pay up. I didn't want them to use me against him like that. I hated it. I was so angry. When they were ready to make the exchange, I didn't just walk to the car like I was supposed to. I jumped on the guy who was with me. His gun went off." He sucked in a deep breath and then blew it out slowly. "He died. My dad's men started shooting at the other guy—Morales, but he got away. We thought that was the end of it, but Morales was out for vengeance. The one who died was his younger brother. He swore to find me and kill me. So, ever since then, I've kept moving. I've stayed away from home—from my dad—and I've kept a low profile. Whenever I've thought that maybe he'd given up, there'd be reports of him in the area. And we'd decide that it was time for me to move on again. Go hide somewhere new." He looked down into her eyes. "But I don't want to move on again. I don't want to hide anymore. I don't want to start a new life in a new place. I want to live my life here, with you."

Maria reached up and landed a kiss on his lips. "That's what I want, too, Zack. But if it means keeping you safe, I'll go somewhere new with you."

He closed his arms around her and hugged her tight. "That means more than you know. But it wouldn't work. It's time to face him. To end this."

Maria's heart was racing. "How can it end?"

"Either he'll get me, or I'll get him."

"Can't the police—this FBI man, Manny—can't he get him?"

Zack made a face. "I'd love to think so, but he hasn't managed it yet."

~ ~ ~

Zack was pouring Maria a mug of coffee when his phone rang.

"Is that Manny?" asked Maria.

He nodded. "Yeah. Let's see what he has to say." He swiped to answer. "Morning."

"Hey, Zack. We arrived a couple of hours ago and started asking around. He's here. We have a handful of positive IDs."

"Well, at least we know for sure."

"We do. I'd rather you weren't here—but I know I'm not going to be able to persuade you to leave," he added hurriedly before Zack could argue.

"That's right."

"So, what exactly are you thinking?"

Zack pursed his lips. He hadn't made a plan yet. He hadn't been thinking straight last night. Not since he'd realized that that bastard might have been in Maria's back yard while she was home alone. "I think I should go about my business as usual. If he's finally found me, it shouldn't take long for him to make his move."

"Okay, and what is your business as usual?"

Zack thought about it. "Well. I'm not working, so I'm not flying. All I've been doing is hanging out during the day while Maria's at work and then spending the evenings with her."

"But she's not gone to work."

Zack glanced out the window. "Are you outside?"

"Not me, no. I've set up base in the resort in town."

"So, how about I bring Maria down there for breakfast?"

"Are you sure you want to get her involved?"

Zack glanced at her. She was watching him curiously. "She's already involved. If anything, I want you to help me persuade her to maybe leave town until this is over."

"Okay. Bring her down here with you."

~ ~ ~

They got into Zack's truck in the garage before he pushed the remote to open the door. She smiled at him. "This is like the movies. Should I get down on the floor, so no one sees me?"

He didn't laugh as he looked back at her. "You know, that's not a bad idea."

As Maria slid down from her seat and crouched in the footwell, her heart was racing. "The only way I can deal with this is to pretend that we're just joking around."

He gave her a wry smile as he pulled out of the driveway. "Okay, then. Let's pretend it's a joke."

She laughed. "It has to be. I'm not the kind of girl you'd find down here normally."

He raised an eyebrow but kept his eyes on the road. She reached over and touched the front of his pants. "The kind of girl you could get to crouch in the footwell of your truck."

He let out a small laugh. "Nor would I want you to be. But you'd better stop that before we get to town, or I might have to take a detour down a quiet lane and get you to demonstrate exactly what you're talking about."

She laughed. "One day, when this is all behind us, I should do that."

She watched his lips twitch into a smile. "That might not be a bad way to celebrate."

"Am I supposed to stay down here the whole way to town?"

"No. Come on up now. You probably didn't need to get down there anyway, but when you suggested it, I thought it might not be a bad idea. This way, if he's watching the house, he won't know that you spent the night."

Maria scrambled back up into the seat. "And why does that matter?"

"It matters because if he knows how close we are, he'll want to hurt you. As far as he's concerned, I killed the person he cared about most in the world."

Maria nodded as she followed the logic. "So, he might want to kill someone he thinks you care about?"

"The person I care about most in the world."

Her heart raced to hear him say that. "What about your dad? Has he never gone after him?" She had to ask that; she couldn't think that she might be the person Zack cared most about. That was too big to deal with yet.

"He might have tried. But there's no way he could ever get close. My dad lives on a big estate on the coast. He's surrounded by security twenty-four seven. Not just because of Morales, it's a result of his business over the years. When we lived in Medellín he … he's a good man …"

Maria nodded. She didn't want to ask what the *but* might be, and it sounded like there was one.

"I want you to meet him," Zack continued. "Would you consider going down there—to stay with him?"

She frowned. "When? I thought you wanted to be here."

"I do. I mean, would you go?"

"No." She knew he meant well, but there was no way she was going to leave the lake and go and hide. Especially not now. "When this is over with, I'd like for us to go and visit. I'd love to meet him. But I want to be here with you."

Zack nodded. "Let's see what Manny has to say."

Ben, who owned the resort, greeted them with a smile when they entered the restaurant. "Manny's over at the lodge. He asked me to tell you to go straight up to room 222."

Maria felt nervous as Zack knocked on the door when they got there. He put his arm around her shoulders and hugged her into his side. "You'll like Manny. He's a good man. He'll do everything in his power to keep you safe."

"What about you?"

He nodded. "Me, too."

The man who opened the door wasn't what she expected. He was dressed in jeans and a T-shirt, not a black suit and white shirt. He hurried them in and closed the door behind them before he embraced Zack. "It's good to see you."

"You too. It's been a long time. I'd like you to meet Maria."

Manny almost crushed her hand when he shook it. She liked him immediately. "Nice to meet you."

He smiled. "And you. I just wish it were under different circumstances. Has Zack talked to you about leaving town?"

"He has, but I don't want to. I want to be here, and besides, I have a job. I can't just up and leave."

Manny sighed. "I had a feeling you were going to say that. If you're going to stay here, you're going to have to get used to having one of these guys following you around at all times."

She looked to the sofa where two more men were sitting. They smiled and nodded but didn't speak.

"Okay."

Manny turned to Zack. "You, too. I'm going to have someone on you."

Zack frowned. "You don't think he'll spot them? I want to draw him out, not scare him off."

"And I want to keep you alive. Give them some credit. They'll stay out of the way. And if I know you, you've already thought of a way to draw him out ... so tell me?"

Maria watched, puzzled. That seemed like an odd thing to say. Why would Manny think that he knew Zack so well? That he knew what he was thinking?

Zack shrugged. "I don't have a plan, as such. But I believe that if I get on with my life, it won't take him long to make his move."

"But you don't have a routine here?"

"No."

"Well, maybe you need one."

Zack nodded. "Yeah. I'll come up with a schedule of what I'm going to do every day—do the same thing at the same time every day. You guys will know it all in advance and he'll be able to figure out when will be his best opportunity. In fact, we should probably work one in there—something that will seem like an easy hit."

Maria shuddered. The word hit made her think of hit men and murders.

Manny smiled at her. "It's okay. He's good at this. So are we."

Zack put his arm around her shoulders. "It'll all be okay. It'll be over soon."

She could only hope so.

Manny turned to Zack. "How would you feel about us staying with you—since Maria's not leaving."

Zack looked down at her, and to her surprise, he nodded slowly. "You probably should."

Maria didn't like that idea at all, and her face must have shown it. "It won't be for long," Zack reassured her. A big smile spread across his face. "In fact, it might be a very good thing."

"How?" she asked doubtfully.

"How would you feel about moving in with me—officially?"

Her heart started to race. "We've only been seeing each other for a couple of weeks." She wanted to kick herself as soon as the words were out. They might have only been seeing each other for a very short time, but she already knew that he was the one for her. What did the timing matter?

Zack was nodding, disappointment etched into the lines around his eyes. "You're right. I'm sorry. I ..."

She smiled at him. "But we've known each other for a long time."

His smile returned. "Is that a yes?"

"It is." Why not? They hadn't spent a night apart since they'd started seeing each other. She hated the idea of sleeping alone again. If he wanted her to move in with him then she'd be happy to.

"Okay. Then we need to spend the day house-hunting."

"House hunting? Why? One of us can move in with the other."

"We could. But now that I'm not hiding anymore, I think I want a nicer place." He smiled at Manny. "Maybe a place with a decent security system and lots of room for guests."

Manny smiled back at him. "Is that an invitation?"

Zack looked down at Maria. "As long as my lady's okay with it."

Maria nodded. She wasn't sure what she was getting herself into, but as long as it meant she got to be with Zack, she was okay with it.

Chapter Thirteen

Zack checked the rearview mirror when he pulled up in front of the gate. Manny had told him he'd be following, but he was too good at it for Zack to spot him. The only vehicle Zack had seen behind them was Austin, the realtor who was now pulling up next to them.

Austin got out of his car and came to Zack's window. "I have to tell you, you took me by surprise on this one."

Zack grinned at him. "It all just kind of came together, and we don't see any reason to wait." He reached across and took hold of Maria's hand. "We know what we want, now we just want to get on with it."

Austin grinned at them. "Hey, congratulations, is all I can say. I'll help you find a place where I hope you'll be very happy together. I brought you out here first, because it matches everything on your wish list, right down to the closed-circuit security system. It's funny, when Clay bought his place, I had a lot of sellers wanting to add camera systems and beef up the security features on their properties. I think they're hoping that other celebrities might want to move here and will be looking for that kind of thing. Though, I'm sure they won't mind that you're not celebrities."

"Celebrities aren't the only people who value their privacy," said Zack.

"Apparently not," agreed Austin. He handed Zack a brochure. "These are all the details on this place. It's well under your budget—both on rent and on listing price, if you decide you want to buy it."

Maria squeezed his hand tightly and he noticed that she was looking at the price with wide eyes. He slid the brochure into the door pocket and nodded. He wanted to tell Austin he was more interested in finding the right property than in how much it cost, but he didn't want to say that in front of Maria. Money wasn't an issue for him, and he was hoping it wouldn't be one for her either.

"Let's get in there and take a look then." He squeezed Maria's hand. "See if the lady approves."

She seemed to approve very much as they followed Austin down the long driveway. She stared out the window at the lake. It was the perfect spring day—just right for a new beginning, he couldn't help thinking. The sky was a pale blue, dotted with white clouds, and the lake reflected the colors in its wind-ruffled surface. The first spring flowers brightened the flower-beds set into the manicured lawns that swept down to the water's edge.

When they pulled up in front of the house, Zack had to laugh at the look on Maria's face. "Do you want to go see inside?"

She shook her head as if to clear it. "Is this some kind of joke?"

"Hell, no! I've never been more serious about anything in my life!"

Austin came to his window, making Zack realize that he was standing there waiting to take them inside and show them around. "Come see it with me? If you don't like it—if it's too much, we'll find something else."

Maria looked uncertain, but she nodded and climbed out of the truck.

Austin grinned at them. "I'll let you in and leave you to it. You guys look around, see what you think. I'll be out here if you have any questions."

"Thanks." Zack was grateful Austin didn't want to give them the tour. He wanted to have Maria to himself while they looked around. He could see it was a lot for her to take in.

~ ~ ~

Maria went straight through to the living room and stood looking out of the windows at the amazing view of the lake. She looked over her shoulder when Zack came to stand behind her and rested his hands on her hips.

"Do you want to do this?" He spoke next to her ear, his warm breath sending shivers chasing each other down her spine.

She shook her head and blew out a sigh. "Which bit?"

He slid his arms around her waist and held her back against him. "Any of it."

She rested her head against his shoulder and looked up into his eyes. "I want to do you."

He smiled and landed a kiss on her lips. "I want to do you, too, but I think we should maybe wait until the place is ours."

She made a face at him. "You know what I mean. I want to be with you. I like the idea of moving in with you—it's fast, but it's not like we don't know each other well enough. But I thought you meant at your place, or mine. Not something like this." She swung her arm out to indicate the huge great room with its view of the lake, and the open loft above.

"You don't like it?"

She had to laugh. "I love it! But it's so … so … big, so much. I never … I don't …" She blew out a sigh. "Zack. We know each other fairly well, but just like I didn't know your history, you don't know mine. I grew up in a freaking trailer park. All my family still live there. I never expected to live somewhere like this. I don't need all this."

He held her gaze for a long moment and she was worried she'd offended him. This was no doubt what he was used to, maybe what he'd been longing to get back to after all his years in hiding.

"I'm sorry."

"Please, don't be! I must sound horrible. I'm not saying no, I'm just saying that if you're doing this for me, you don't need to." She cupped his face between her hands and kissed him. "All I want is to be with you."

He smiled. "And that's all I want, too. I admit it, I do want to be able to give us a nice home, but I'll go with whatever your idea of nice is—afterward. The reason I want to look at places like this right now is only partly to impress you and maybe sweep you off your feet."

She felt bad when he gave her a sad smile. "I seem to have failed at that. But a house like this will be really useful for the next few weeks, at least. Hopefully not much longer. The whole place is monitored by a CCTV system. There's room for

Manny and his guys to stay in one wing of the house and be on hand if we need them, without having them in our space. I don't see us spending the evenings sitting in front of the TV in your living room with them—do you?"

She shook her head. "No, of course. I get it. I'm sorry. I didn't mean to be … whatever, about this place. It's beautiful, and of course, you're right. It's perfect for what you need. That's what matters."

He hugged her to him. "You're what matters. Everything else is just detail. Big house or small house. Dead or alive. None of it matters if I'm not with you."

She squeezed her arms tight around his waist. "Don't you dare say that. Dead or alive matters. It always matters."

He nodded. "You're right. It does. It matters a whole lot more since I met you."

She smiled up at him. "It does to me, too. I don't have anyone out to get me or anything, and I was happy with my life before. But now we're together, I'm looking forward to how great life can be—once we get this crazy man of yours taken care of." She looked around at the beautiful house. "And if us living here for a while can help you take care of him once and for all, then I suppose I can put up with it."

He chuckled. "I'm glad you can put a positive spin on it."

She made a face at him. "It's not exactly hard. It's an amazing house."

He nodded. "I like it. Let's look around a bit more, and if you think you're okay with it, we'll tell Austin we'll take it."

Maria nodded. "How long of a lease do they want?"

Zack shrugged. "I don't know. I'll ask him."

Zack watched her wander around the kitchen, opening drawers and peeking inside the fridge while he stood with Manny in the great room. The house was perfect for what he'd been thinking of. When Manny had asked this morning if he and the guys could stay with them it had given him a game plan. His primary objective was to keep Maria safe. Having the guys stay with them would go a long way to making sure that happened. Like he'd told Maria, there was no way he could see the guys coming to stay at either of their places. But moving in to a place like this would mean that he and Maria could finally be open about the fact that they were together—not just together but living together. Once people knew that, Morales would think Zack was getting careless, and would no doubt think it was time to make his move. He just hoped that Manny and the guys were being careful enough about not making their presence known. In a place like this it'd be easier to keep them out of sight than if they were coming and going on his street or Maria's. What he hadn't told her was the reason he'd wanted to see this particular property first. Yes, there was the big front gate and the long driveway, like most of the other properties on this section of the waterfront, but there was also a back entrance. A lane that came through the woods and led to a gate on the back of the property. That would allow Manny and the guys to come and go, while he and Maria appeared to be the only ones using the front gate.

Manny raised an eyebrow at him. "It all looks good to me."

"And you all came in the back way?"

"No, the guys did. I followed you."

"I didn't see you."

Manny smirked at him. "Did you expect to?"

Zack smiled. "I half hoped."

"You should know better than that. So, are you going to tell Austin that you'll take the place?"

"I am."

"Good, and then we need to get to work, setting up a routine that you can follow every day. Can you think of anything that would be a natural weak point? A time and a place that would make it easy for him to make his move?"

Zack shook his head. "I can't. Honestly, right now, I can't focus on all that. First, I need to get this place locked in with Austin and then I need to spend some time with Maria. She says she's okay with it, but it's a lot to take in. And ... before we move in here, she's going to want to tell people—so am I, for that matter. It's time we went public."

"Are you sure you want to do that?"

Zack nodded. "I've wanted to do it ever since I started seeing her. It's important to me. I want the world to know— for my sake, and more importantly for hers. I don't want her to feel like I'm keeping her hidden away. She needs to know how proud I am that she wants to be with me."

Manny smiled. "I always wondered if it would come down to this."

"To what?"

"You've stayed in hiding for a long time. I know you didn't want to, but you did it for your dad."

Zack nodded. "He's never gotten over the guilt he feels that they took me. They took me to get to his money. He feels like it's all his fault. I never saw it that way. It was all down to them and the choices they made. They chose to become criminals. It's not Dad's fault, but it still eats him up. If it were just for me, I would have gone about my life and taken my chances, but I know that if Morales had found me and killed me, it would have killed my dad, too. He wanted me to stay hidden—to stay safe—so I've done that all these years for him."

"But now, because of Maria, you can't do it anymore. It's taken the love of a good woman. She's the one for you, isn't she?"

Zack nodded. "She is." He glanced over at her again, wondering if she knew that—and why he hadn't told her yet.

She caught him watching her and looked a little guilty as she closed the dishwasher.

"Today is her only day off this week. I want to go sign the paperwork with Austin and then take her to get our things so we can spend the night here. She's back at work in the morning. Can we wait till then to go over my new routine?"

"Sure," said Manny. "It can wait. The guys and I can get set up around here. The mother-in-law apartment is perfect. We'll be here with you but not on top of you."

"Exactly."

~ ~ ~

As they wandered up and down the aisles of the grocery store, Maria kept looking back over her shoulder.

"Are you okay?" asked Zack.

She smiled up at him. "Yes, sorry. I should make it less obvious, shouldn't I? I just find it hard to believe that one of Manny's guys is here. I haven't spotted him once."

Zack smiled. "That's how it's supposed to be."

"I know, but I always thought it was so far-fetched. You see it on movies, but I thought that in real life, you'd spot them. I didn't think people could be that sneaky."

"People can be very sneaky."

Her smile faded. "I hope Morales isn't as good at it as they are."

"He's managed to avoid them for all this time."

Maria couldn't think about that—about the scary reality. She shook her head. "Yes, but they haven't been looking for him full time and expecting him like they are now. They didn't know where he was most of the time and he wasn't around you."

"True." He slung his arm around her shoulders. "Hopefully, it'll all be over soon."

She shrugged his arm off in a panic. "We're not supposed to …" and then she stopped. "But we can now, can't we?"

He smiled. "We can. If you want to. I want to shout it from the rooftops and tell everyone that we're together—that we're so together that you're moving in with me."

Her heart started to race.

"You don't want to tell everyone?"

"I do, but I need to tell my family. They'll want to meet you. They'll have all kinds of questions, they'll want to know…" She stopped herself. She could hardly tell him that her parents wouldn't be happy about them living together because they'd expect them to at least be engaged first. When she was younger, a young couple moving in together was seen as a terrible thing—it brought shame on the family. Over the years, thanks to all her cousins, her family had accepted that it happened—but only if the couple planned to marry. It was acceptable if they were engaged and saving for their wedding.

"What?" Zack was watching her, waiting for her to finish the sentence.

"They'll want to know all about you. They're old-fashioned. I don't think they'll approve of us moving in together."

He held her gaze for a long moment. She wished she knew what was going on behind those big brown eyes. "Not unless I plan to marry you?"

Her tummy flipped over as she nodded. She didn't know what he meant by that half smile he gave her. Was he thinking that was a ridiculous idea—that they were just enjoying something casual, if you could live with someone casually? Maybe that's all it was to him. Or was he sympathizing that she had such old-fashioned parents? Or ...what? She didn't know and she felt stupid.

"I look forward to meeting them."

She smiled. At least, he wasn't put off by it, or saying anything about how behind the times they were. She nodded. Hoping that someday he would meet them.

While they stood in line at the checkout, Maria looked around again. She was still wondering if she might spot one of Manny's men, but she was also wondering if anyone might spot her and Zack together. He was holding her hand, not hiding that they were together.

Her question was answered when she heard Roxy's not so dulcet tones calling her name. "Maria!"

She waved to her friend who had just finished paying for her groceries a couple of lines over. She came and stood next to the cashier and grinned. "Well, aren't you two cute? And what's all this?" She looked into the bags and at the items the cashier was ringing up. "This looks like more than dinner for two, this look like several dinners for two. Is there anything you want to tell me?"

Maria looked up at Zack. He'd said they could tell their friends, but had he meant so openly, in the middle of the grocery store?

Apparently, he had. He smiled at her and then at Roxy. "You're right, there's everything we need for dinner for two for the next week, till we come grocery shopping again."

Roxy's eyes grew wide as she smiled at him.

"In fact, we also bought enough for guests, since we were thinking about inviting you and Angel and Luke and the guys over to our new place this weekend."

Roxy's mouth fell open, but she recovered quickly. "Run that one by my again. Did you just say *our* new place?"

Zack nodded at her and Maria grinned.

"Oh, my God! Please tell me I helped you along? I know I was out of order that night at Angel's telling you I couldn't share the taxi, but it was only because I wanted to help get you two together."

Maria laughed. "You did help. Thank you."

Zack grinned. "Yeah, I owe you one—big time. I shall be forever grateful."

Roxy grinned back at him. "You don't owe me a damned thing. You just made me so happy!" She looked at Maria. "But moving in together, so quickly?"

Maria nodded. "We both know it's what we want, so why not?"

Roxy clasped her hands together. "Why not indeed. You go for it, guys. I have to get out of here. I'm working the night shift tonight, but call me, okay? Oh, wait, no. I'll see you on Thursday. You can tell me all about it then."

She left just as the cashier got finished. Maria pulled her purse out and beat Zack to it. He frowned at her, but she just smiled. "I pay my way, Mister. You'd better get used to it." She was relieved that he smiled and accepted it graciously. He was going to have to let her do what she could. She'd seen how much the rent was for the house, and there was no way she could afford that!

Chapter Fourteen

Zack knew he would always remember that first night they spent in the house. When they got back from the store, he and Maria put the groceries away. It didn't feel strange to him to be in a new kitchen, figuring out between the two of them where they wanted things to go. It felt right. He'd lived in so many different places, but this didn't feel like just one more. It felt like he was finally making a home.

Maria closed the fridge and came over to slide her arms around his waist. "What's up? You look lost in thought. You're not regretting this already, are you?"

He rested his hands on her shoulders and landed a kiss on her lips. "No. I'm not regretting it at all. Just the opposite, in fact." She looked up into his eyes and he tangled his fingers in her long, dark hair. "I was thinking that of all the times I've moved, of all the new places I've set myself up in, this one is the best." He wanted to say he hoped it would be the last, too, but he knew she was a little uncomfortable with such a big house. He hoped it would grow on her, but it wasn't the house that was making him feel like he'd finally found his home. It was her.

She smiled. "It is an amazing place. I didn't mean that I don't like it earlier. It's just a bit grander than I'm used to."

He hugged her to his chest. "I know. And I'm not thinking that it's the best because it's big or because it's so nice. It's the best, because you're here. I love this place, because it's our place." He looked down into her eyes. He wanted to tell her that it wasn't even about loving the house—it was because he loved her.

She smiled. "I love that we're doing this, Zack. I really do. It's hard to believe that only a few weeks ago you were still just my crush, my friend. I used to have to ask Angel to find out when you were coming back to town. Now we're here." She looked around. "This is our home. For now, at least."

"It can be our home for as long as you want it to be."

She nodded. "I guess we have to see what happens first, don't we? I'm trying not to think too hard about why we're really here. I'm trying not to think about Manny and the others being just on the other side of that wall, and most of all, I'm trying not to let myself think about the fact that there's a man—here in Summer Lake—who wants to kill you."

"I don't want you to think about it. I want you to enjoy this. I'm hoping it will all be over soon."

"So am I, but I wish there was something I could do."

"That's how I've felt all these years. I wished that I could put an end to it one way or another. Now, the end is in sight. Manny's here; his guys are the best. It's only a matter of time before Morales makes his move."

Her eyes filled up with tears. "But what if he succeeds? What if ...? I can't stand the thought of anything happening to you, Zack."

He hugged her tight. "Nothing's going to happen to me. They'll take him down before he gets the chance."

She sniffed and looked up at him. "They better had. I'm not going to lose you now."

"You won't. You're stuck with me." He had an overwhelming urge to add, *for life*, but he stopped himself. He didn't want to tempt fate by telling her that and having his own life not last much longer. And besides, he hadn't even told her that he loved her yet. He grinned. "And just so that you know that being stuck with me is going to be a good thing, I'm going to make you dinner."

She smiled. "You don't have to do it all, I can help."

"You can help, but what I want you to do is go and get dressed. Get dressed up as if you were going out on a first date."

She gave him a puzzled look.

"I never got to take you out to a nice restaurant. We never got to have a first date. We should do that. I don't want us to just slip into TV dinners. I want to make the most of all the butterflies and excitement that go with the early days of dating."

She smiled. "That's sweet. How did you know that you give me butterflies?"

He touched her cheek. "I was talking about you giving me butterflies."

"Aww." She landed a kiss on his lips. "You keep talking like that and we'll have to pretend it's at least a fourth or fifth date."

"Why's that?"

She laughed. "Because you're going to charm me right into bed and there's no way I'd sleep with you on a first date."

He shook his head. "Maybe we should call it a first and find out how persuasive I can be." He ran his hand down her back and closed it around her ass.

She shook her head. "Don't start that. I'm going to get changed. Otherwise, there'll be no date at all, just humping in the kitchen."

He had to laugh. "Okay. Tempting as that sounds, it's not what I had in mind. Go get dressed before I change my mind."

~ ~ ~

Maria sat at the dressing table in front of the mirror and smiled at herself. This place was amazing. She'd just taken the best shower she'd ever had. The shower stall was bigger than her laundry room at home and there were four shower heads—on each side. She couldn't wait to get Zack in there with her. Now she was getting ready in her own dressing room—she wasn't so keen on that idea—Zack's was on the other side of the huge closet. She'd rather share with him.

She finished putting on her makeup. She was going all out—making as much effort as she would if this really were their first date. This past few weeks, ever since they'd started seeing each other had been so strange. His situation had overshadowed everything. They'd come together faster than they would have if there weren't some crazy man out there wanting to kill him. She shuddered and shoved that thought away. She wasn't going to let it spoil tonight. This was their first night in the home they shared—and according to Zack, it was their first real date, too.

She hadn't had to spend long deciding what to wear. She'd spent so much time over the last year thinking about Zack and about how it would be if he ever asked her out. She'd even picked out what she would wear if he ever did. She slipped the dress on over her head and let out a low whistle. Yep. This was it, and if she knew Zack, tonight would definitely be more like a fifth date than a first one. The dress came down to her mid calves; it was form-fitting, to say the least. The front was cut low enough that she knew he'd spend more time talking to her breasts than her face. She turned around and smiled at the way it showed off her backside. Yes. It was perfect. She ran the brush through her hair again. She used to imagine that she'd wear her hair up for their first date. But now she knew better. He liked her hair down and loose. He liked to tangle his fingers in it. She took a deep breath and brought herself back to the present. She couldn't think too much about how he liked to hold her hair in bed, or they'd never make it through dinner. It was strange to her to let a man cook for her. Her family was more traditional. She'd grown up knowing only old school gender roles, but she loved that Zack didn't expect her to be that way.

She turned at the sound of footsteps on the stairs. "It's only me," he called. "I'm going to take a quick shower. Everything's ready, and I poured you a drink if you go down before me."

"Where are you?" His voice was coming from the other side of the bedroom.

He laughed. "I'm in my dressing room. Play along with me? I want to get changed and come find my beautiful date."

She chuckled. "Okay. I'm done here. I'll go downstairs and wait for you there."

"I won't be long."

She found a glass of red wine sitting on the counter with a note next to it. "I can't wait to see you again."

She laughed and took a sip of her wine and then carried her glass over to the big picture windows overlooking the lake. It was staying lighter much longer now. She was grateful that spring was finally here. The winters weren't exactly harsh at the lake, but she much preferred the warmer weather, and she loved seeing all the flowers starting to bloom.

She turned when the door from the other side of the house opened. Manny popped his head around and smiled at her. "Sorry. I don't mean to interrupt."

"You're not," she said with a smile. "Zack's just taking a shower."

Manny frowned. "He didn't tell me you're going out."

"We're not."

Manny looked her over.

"Oh!" She shrugged. "We're having a date night at home."

"Ah. Okay. Sorry. I just came to ask what time you're leaving for work in the morning."

Maria made a face. "I'm not sure. I think I'll need to add an extra ten minutes onto what it usually takes me, and I usually leave around nine … soo …"

Manny gave her a reassuring smile. "I'm not trying to pin you down to an exact time. I just want a ballpark so one of the guys can be ready to go."

She nodded. She hadn't exactly forgotten about all that, but she'd been doing her best not to think about it. "Are you going to be able to keep him safe?"

Manny pursed his lips. "I'm going to do my damnedest. I wish I could promise you. But I'll do everything in my power."

"Thank you."

Manny came in and closed the door behind him. "Aren't you scared?"

Maria sighed. "I know I should be, but it's all ... I don't know. It doesn't feel real, and I can't let myself think about it too much. I just have to hope that between you and Zack you'll be able to catch this man and keep Zack safe."

"That's the plan, but I meant, aren't you scared for yourself? You're a good-looking girl. I'm sure there are lots of guys who'd like to take you out. Wouldn't it be easier to date someone who doesn't have Zack's kind of history?"

Maria frowned. She didn't get it. She liked Manny; she'd thought he liked her. Was he trying to tell her to get out—for her own sake? "I'm not scared for myself. Zack seems to think I should be, but I'm more concerned about him."

Manny held up a hand. "I'm sorry. I just need to know."

"Know what?"

"How you really feel. You're in this for keeps, aren't you?"

She nodded.

Manny smiled. "I'm glad. I know how Zack feels about you. You feel the same way, don't you?"

Although she answered, "Yes," Maria wasn't sure that it was true. She knew Zack cared about her. She knew he wanted to see where things could go between the two of them. But she wasn't sure that she felt the same way as him. She had a feeling that she was already way ahead of him. She was falling in love with him; if she was honest, she'd already fallen.

"That's all I wanted to know. Zack's decisions are going to be clouded by how he feels. I needed to know that he's not making a mistake."

They both looked up as Zack came down the stairs.

Maria's breath caught in her chest. She'd always thought he might be the sexiest man she'd ever known. Tonight, her suspicion was confirmed. He looked gorgeous!

"Is there a problem?" he asked Manny.

"No. I was just checking what time Maria has to leave for work in the morning."

Zack nodded. "I can take you, if you like? We should probably leave a little before nine."

"Thanks. If you want to come, that'll be great. But I'm fine to drive myself."

"I'd rather you stayed here," said Manny. "The sooner we can get a plan together, the better."

Zack met Maria's gaze. "Are you sure?"

She laughed. "I'm sure. I've driven myself to work almost every day of my life since I was sixteen. I can handle it."

Zack nodded and Manny laughed. "You might as well accept it, Zack. You wouldn't have fallen in love with her if she were some needy little damsel."

Maria's heart raced. They were just words. Manny didn't mean them. He didn't know how Zack felt. He was just ... She turned to Zack and he looked at her in that way he had—the one she'd never been able to figure out.

The silence between them dragged out for a few moments before Manny broke it. "Okay. I'll see you both in the morning. Have a good night."

It was only once the door had closed behind him that Zack came to her. He put his hands on her hips and let his gaze travel over her. "Damn, Maria, *mía*. If I'd known you were going to wear that dress on our first date, I would have caved and asked you out a long time ago."

She laughed. "Now he tells me." She reached up and landed a kiss on his lips. "And if I'd have known that you would look this good and ..." She nuzzled her face into his neck. "... smell this good, I would have asked you out myself."

He closed his arms around her. "I don't believe in fate, but I believe we make the choices that fit who we are at the time we make them. I wish I could go back in time so we could have gotten together sooner, but we're here now, and I know this is right. It's what I want. Is it what you want?"

She nodded as she hugged him closer. It seemed liked a strange question. She wouldn't be here if it wasn't what she wanted.

~ ~ ~

Zack closed his eyes as he held her soft, warm body to his chest. Manny had almost blown it—saying that he wouldn't have fallen in love with her if she weren't the strong woman that she was. Zack wanted to be the one to tell her that he was in love with her. The way she'd looked at him when Manny said that had hardly reassured him. Maybe this was going too fast for her. Maybe he should wait. There was no hurry, was there?

He buried his face in her neck, breathing in the scent of her. He was in a hurry. He'd wasted so much time that they could have been together. And, much as he hated to think about it, there was a chance that he didn't have much time left. He was confident in Manny and his men; he was confident in his own abilities if it came down to it, but he didn't doubt Morales either. Just because he hadn't caught up with Zack in all this time didn't mean anything. Zack believed that Morales had intentionally let it go on for such a long time. He wasn't looking for swift vengeance; he was more like a cat toying with his prey. He'd kept Zack on the run for most of his adult life. From what Zack remembered of him, he probably enjoyed thinking that Zack was living in fear. He closed his eyes tighter and hugged Maria a little closer. He was afraid to die now. Now he was on the cusp of beginning a whole new life—a life with Maria—filled with love and happiness. He needed to tell her.

She stepped back and looked up into his eyes.

"Do you understand the question?"

She searched his face. "I think so. You're asking if I'm good with us moving in together and …" She shrugged. "Doing this."

He shook his head. "I'm asking so much more than that. But perhaps I shouldn't be asking until you have all the information you need to make a decision."

"What information do I need?"

He smiled and took hold of both of her hands. "Just a couple important details. Before you can decide if this is what you want, you need to know that I'm not just talking about us living here together for a little while until this whole thing is behind us. I'm talking about you making a long-term commitment to live with me—to us being together, for the long haul."

She smiled and nodded.

"The most important thing you need to know is that I love you."

Her eyes shone with tears. "You do?"

He closed his arms around her waist and nodded. "I do. My heart knew it from the start, but I couldn't …" He shrugged. "I thought I could hide how I felt, but I can't do it anymore. I love you too much to keep hiding it."

She reached up and cupped his face between her hands. "I love you, too, Zack. You're the most amazing man I've ever known. You have no idea how happy I am to know you feel it, too."

He lowered his head and brushed his lips over hers. The way she kissed him back left him with no doubts. Right from the beginning, he'd loved the way she kissed him. She was so warm and inviting, so sweet and so passionate. She pressed herself against him and he knew she must feel how much she turned him on.

Eventually, he stepped back with a smile. "We should probably cool it, if this is our first date."

She laughed. "That's a shame. I thought you were just showing me how persuasive you can be."

He smiled through pursed lips.

"And just so you know, I'm persuaded."

He looked at her, then into the kitchen where the dinner he'd prepared for her was all ready to be served. He was tempted to lead her straight up the stairs, but instead, he took her hand and led her to the kitchen. "Let's do this right."

She gave him a rueful smile. "If you insist, but be warned, I'm not above doing some persuading myself."

He let his gaze run over her. "I'm in."

Chapter Fifteen

Maria looked around when she came out of the store. She knew that one of Manny's men would be there, but she couldn't see him anywhere. Then again, she wasn't supposed to. All she was supposed to do was go about her business as usual. Tonight, that meant having dinner with the girls. She and Angel were meeting at the café in the plaza as soon after six as they could both get there. The other girls were coming over from town to meet them at seven.

She couldn't help wondering if someone was watching her as she made her way down the cobbled walkway that led from the jewelry story to the square. There were still a few people around, although most of the stores closed at six. Laura had told her to leave a little early and that she'd lock up. Maria wasn't sure there was much point—Angel wasn't one to leave work early no matter what, so she'd have to sit and wait for her. But still, this way Laura had let her out of the front door, so she didn't have to walk around the back.

She was pleased to see that the terrace of the café was still open. The days were getting warmer and it was lasting into the evening now. She loved to sit outside to eat.

"Hey, Maria."

She jumped when a man called her name and looked around wondering who it was. She relaxed and waved when she saw Colt sitting on the far side of the terrace. "Hey, how are you?" she asked when she reached him.

"I'm fine thanks. Just making the most of my day off. I brought myself over here for dinner for a change. How about you? Did you just get off work? Are you meeting Zack?"

"I did just finish, but I'm here to meet Angel. We're having dinner with the girls later."

Colt smiled. "Are you leaving him home alone already?"

She laughed. "No. He's hanging out with Luke. In fact, he's probably glad to get an evening away from me."

"I doubt that. I could tell he liked you ever since he first came here. I'm happy for both of you that you finally got it together—and it sounds like you're making up for lost time. I heard you moved in together and everything."

She nodded. "Yeah. It's all happening a bit fast, but it's not like we don't already know each other well."

"I wasn't criticizing. Like I said, I'm happy for you. I think it's great."

"What about you? Are you seeing anyone?"

He shook his head. "Nah. Austin set me up on a date with one of Nadia's friends a couple of weeks ago, but …"

"Ugh." She immediately brought her hand up to cover her mouth. It wasn't like her to be so rude.

Colt laughed. "Don't worry about it. That's how I felt. I don't get Austin with Nadia. She's just not … I don't know. I was going to say our kind of people. But what kind of people are we? We're an eclectic bunch if you think about it. You and Zack aren't exactly peas in a pod, yet it's so obvious that you're meant to be together. Angel and Luke are the same. He's so laid back, she's a workaholic and yet they're perfect together. Austin's kind of a workaholic, too, I guess. Roxy's just fun and down to earth. Logan's a dog, no two ways about it. I'm whatever I am. But we all just gel. Whenever Austin brings Nadia along, she disrupts the harmony. She doesn't fit right with the rest of us."

Maria smiled. "Do you want to know how I see it?"

"Yeah."

"I think we all gel because, no matter how different we are on the surface, underneath we're all kind, caring people. You think about the whole bunch of us, and there's not one who wouldn't go out of their way to help someone. Nadia's not like that. She's all about what's in it for her. She doesn't like Austin hanging out with us because we're not the cool kids, we're not the *in* crowd. We're of no value to her because we don't have anything to offer. We're not the wealthy ones, hanging out with us won't help her social standing."

Colt frowned. "Yeah. I can see that, but she doesn't hang out with the people who would elevate her social status either. I mean you think about the people with money around here— and there's a lot of them, with a lot of it—you don't see her hanging out with them either."

Maria smiled. "Because being wealthy doesn't necessarily make you superficial. Some of the most down-to-earth people around here could buy and sell the rest of us. There's Smoke, for starters. And think about Dan Benson. And his brother Jack and Pete Hemming. They're all multi-multi-millionaires, but they're not about all the social climbing and that kind of stuff that Nadia is."

Colt nodded. "You've got a point there. Even if you deliberately didn't mention Zack."

She frowned.

"Okay. Sorry. I'll drop it, but we both know Zack's got more money than the rest of them put together."

She smiled. What else was she supposed to do? She knew Zack's family was wealthy. She knew he had a lot more than she did, but it didn't matter, did it? She wasn't going to let her pride get in the way of the way she felt about him. "I guess he's just another example. I don't even think of him as being one of the money people because that's not who he is to me."

Colt smiled. "It's not who he is to any of us. He's just Zack." The server came out with his food and Maria smiled.

"I'll leave you to your dinner. But if you're here for a while I'll come over when the girls arrive. Lenny's granddaughters are coming. I should introduce you."

Colt smiled. "I'll probably be gone by then."

She laughed. "Stick around. If your dating options are down to Nadia's friends, then it's time you met some new people."

He laughed with her. "You might have a point there. I think Austin likes one of them, though."

Maria frowned. "Well, that's neither here nor there until he breaks up with Nadia, is it?"

"No, but I'm not going to get in the way."

"Hey, you two." Angel appeared at Maria's side.

"Hey." Colt smiled at her. "Go on. You two get your chatting time in before the others arrive. I'll catch up with you both soon."

"Are you working on Saturday?" asked Angel.

"I'm on the early shift this weekend."

"Good. Then you can come out in the evening."

Colt smiled. "I'd love to. Let me know what the plans are."

"Will do. Talk to you soon."

Angel took Maria's arm and led her away. They found a table on the other side of the terrace. "We can move inside later if the girls want to, but let's sit out here for now."

"Sounds good to me. How are you?"

Angel laughed. "I'm fine. Luke's fine. We're very happy together. Work's great and … umm … unless you can think of anything else, that's me done. Now that we're caught up on my news, I want to hear all about you."

Maria laughed. "That's it?"

"Yes! You're the one who's got so much going on. A couple of weeks ago, you were happy to get a glimpse of Zack. Then you were seeing each other but no one could know about it. Now, you're happily living together in one of the big waterfront estates and everyone's talking about it. I think, as your best friend, you owe me a few details here and there to fill in the gaps."

"Well, since you put it like that. I suppose I do."

"So, come on, what happened? How did you go from naught to sixty in no time at all? And don't get me wrong. I'm not giving you a hard time. I'm thrilled. I know how much you like him. I've always suspected how much he liked you, but he's so private. He's been like the mystery man." She grinned. "So, what's it like to unravel the mystery?"

Maria looked around. There was no one sitting close enough to hear them. "I don't mind telling you that he makes me unravel!"

Angel chuckled with her. "I had a feeling he might. He's one of those guys, isn't he? He's all manly and sexy and …" She rolled her eyes. "Not my type. You know that."

"I do know that, and you're right. I always thought of Zack as more of a macho type, but he's so sweet, too, Angel. He's so good to me. He cooks for me and he brings me coffee in bed in the morning before I have to go to work."

"Aww. That's lovely. He can come across a bit harsh. I remember when Luke and I first started seeing each other, he thought I might be just using Luke and he wasn't afraid to say so. But it was only because he cared about his friend."

"Yeah. You wouldn't think of him as a sweetie pie, but he is underneath."

"At least, he is to you, and that's all that matters. So, where do you go from here? I can't believe you just moved into that house together—oh, and by the way, I'll expect you to invite me and Luke over as soon as you're settled."

Maria smiled. "I'd love to."

"What was the big hurry, though?"

She'd asked Zack how much she could tell Angel, and he'd said there was no reason not to tell her everything. He wasn't making any attempt to hide anymore. And he'd already told Luke. "What's Luke told you?"

Angel made a face. "He said Zack finally explained what his situation was and that it made sense to him that the two of you would want to move into a place like that. He said that some guy has been after Zack for years and Zack's sick of running and hiding."

"That's about it," said Maria. She looked around again. She'd been about to tell Angel about Manny, but thought better of it.

"So, you're just waiting for this man to track Zack down so they can have some kind of showdown?"

Maria nodded.

"Do you know what it's all about?"

She nodded again. "I do, and I don't think I want to talk about it here—out in public. I'll tell you when we're on our own."

"Okay. But do I need to worry about you? Luke said that Zack had always liked you, but he'd never done anything about it because he didn't want to put you in danger."

Maria nodded.

"And you aren't in danger now? Why is it safe all of a sudden?"

"Well, for one thing, the house is pretty much a fortress. It's in its own grounds behind big gates. There are all sorts of security systems. And … he's got help now. I really don't want to talk about it out here. But he thinks it's all going to be done with soon."

"Okay, but I'm not thrilled. I mean, you're stuck, aren't you? You can't just go back to your place till this man has been caught."

Maria smiled. "You've got nothing to worry about there. I don't want to go back to my place. Not unless Zack's going with me."

"I see." Angel smiled at her. "So, you like him enough that you can put up with all this weirdness?"

"No, I don't like him enough …"

Angel's eyes widened.

Maria couldn't hold back her smile. "I'm in love with him, and he's in love with me."

"Oh, Maria! That's wonderful! I'm so happy for you. I thought the two of you might be headed in that direction, but … no, you know what? It really isn't that fast, is it? You've known each other for ages. The two of you have hung out as friends. You've been much closer than Luke and I were for the last year, until we got together."

"That's true. You know I always hoped for more, and I always kind of got the feeling he liked me. Now I know that the only reason he didn't do anything about it was because of this whole situation."

"So, he stayed away from you just so that you wouldn't get mixed up in this business of his?"

"Yeah." Maria smiled at her friend. "He told me he had to hide his heart."

"Aww! I'm liking him more with everything I hear about him."

Maria grinned. "Me too."

~ ~ ~

"What time are you expecting Maria home?" asked Manny as he followed Zack up the steps to the front door.

"She said she'd be back by ten."

"I thought you'd stay out later yourself."

Zack shrugged. "It was just a quick drink. Luke and I talk all the time." He opened the front door and Manny waited for him to go in first.

"So, the two of you met up to kill some time while your girls are out?"

Zack gave him a rueful smile. "Yeah. You got me."

"It's nothing to be ashamed of. You're in love with her."

Zack nodded. "I know it's nothing to be ashamed of, but I do feel guilty about the timing. I stayed away from her for over a year. I should have been strong enough to wait until Morales was taken care of."

"Maybe, but you can't change what's happened. You can only make the most of it. And if you want to look on the bright side, you could see it that getting together with her is helping to end this."

"You sound like her; she always finds the bright side."

"It's a useful trait to have, as long as you don't let it blind you to the darker side of things. You need to acknowledge that the darker side exists before you turn away from it and look for the good."

"Yeah, she's realistic enough." He went through to the kitchen and took a beer from the fridge. "Do you want one?"

Manny laughed. "Ask me a different question. You know I want one, but I'm not going to have one."

Zack went and sat on the sofa and put his feet up on the coffee table. Manny sat in the armchair opposite him.

"How long do you think it'll take before he shows himself?"

"My guess is that he'll monitor your movements for a couple of weeks. Get a handle on where you go, what you do, when you're most likely to be vulnerable."

Zack nodded. He knew that much himself. He was just antsy. He wanted it to be over with. "How long can you and the guys stay up here? I mean, I'm glad you're here, and honored that you think I'm worth it, but …"

Manny smiled. "I'm glad we're here, too. We've got a month before we need to reassess. And don't flatter yourself. It's not that you're so important. It's him. He's weaved his way in and out of all the major gangs, families, and cartels since his days in Medellín. He has so much information that could—"

"Wait. You're not saying that they'd cut him a deal, are you?"

Manny shook his head. "My job is to bring him in. What happens to him will be up to the justice system."

"So, you're telling me that he might walk free in return for information?"

Manny shook his head. "If he cuts any kind of deal, his priority is going to be hiding his own ass, not coming after yours."

Zack frowned. "I suppose I've been naïve all this time. I was just thinking of him getting locked up and them throwing away the key."

"And that might be the case. But I don't think you'll need to worry about it. I'm more concerned about getting to him before he gets to you."

"And so am I, if I'm honest. I guess I won't need to worry about anything if he gets to me first."

"We won't let that happen, Zack."

"I'm banking on it."

Chapter Sixteen

Maria finished wiping down the countertop and looked around. Everywhere was clean and neat.

Zack came to stand behind her and slid his arms around her waist. "Relax. It's only Angel and Luke."

She rested her head back against his shoulder and looked up into his eyes. "I know. I don't know what's wrong with me. I'm all panicky and wanting everything to be perfect."

He turned her around and planted a kiss on her lips. Then picked her up and sat her on the island. He rested his hands on either side of her hips and rested his forehead against hers. "What are you panicking about, peanut?"

She laughed. "I am not a peanut!"

He kissed her again. "You are to me; you're my little positive peanut. So, I don't get why you're so wound up about our friends coming over. Is something bothering you? Is there something you're not telling me? Something you're not comfortable with?"

"No!" She slid her arms around his shoulders and drew him closer, so he was standing between her legs. "There really isn't anything. That's why I don't understand why I'm so nervous. They're our friends, they're both happy for us."

"Maybe it's not about them?"

"What do you mean?" The way her heart started to race told her that he might be right. Something else was bothering her on some level, but she didn't know what it was.

"You still haven't talked to your parents, have you?"

Her heart thudded to a halt. That was it. She blew out a sigh. "How did you get so smart?"

"I'm not so smart, but I think I know you pretty well by now. It's been bothering you that you haven't told your parents about us. I understand why you don't want to yet. You want all this behind us before you do, right?"

She nodded. "When I tell them about us, it's going to be tough enough to tell them that I already moved in with you. They're going to ask all kinds of questions and I don't want to lie to them. I don't want to hide from them the fact that there's a crazy man trying to kill you." She let out a little laugh. "I guess it'll be easier to tell them that there was a crazy man, but it's all over."

He smiled. "I can't wait until we can tell them that."

"Me neither. I'm hanging in there, Zack. I'm doing my best to look on the bright side, but it is getting to me."

"I know." He closed his arms around her. "It wasn't fair of me to …"

She put a finger to his lips. "Don't you dare say we shouldn't have gotten together yet. You made me wait long enough."

He bit her finger and sucked the tip of it into his mouth. "I promise I'll never make you wait longer than you want to again. Any time you want me, you tell me."

She made a face at him. "That's not fair. I want you now. But we can't."

He stepped closer and rocked his hips. "We could."

She wrapped her legs around his and rubbed herself against him. "They'll be here any minute."

He nipped at her lips and then kissed her deeply. "If you want me, I'm all yours."

She reluctantly put a hand to his shoulder and pushed him back. "Angel and Luke will be here any minute and then we're going out with everyone later. So, I guess I'll have to wait until bedtime. I do want you, and you'd better still be all mine tonight."

He gave her that look, the one she'd never been able to figure out.

"Is that a maybe?" she asked.

He shook his head with a smile. "That's a definitely. I'll still be all yours tonight, and tomorrow, and for all of your tomorrows. I love you, peanut. When I told you you're stuck with me, I meant it. I'm all yours, you're all mine—forever."

She wrapped her arms around him again and nuzzled her face into his neck. "I want to be. I love you so much."

She loosened her grip on him at the sound of the buzzer that told them there was someone at the front gate. Zack went over to check the monitors. "They're here. Manny must have let them in."

~ ~ ~

It had been an enjoyable afternoon. Zack hoped that they'd have many more weekends like this. He hadn't thought he'd ever become one of those guys who was part of a couple and had couple friends. Not only was it not in the cards for him because of his past, but it hadn't held any appeal anyway. Now he understood it. He and Maria had had a great time with Luke and Angel. They'd all been friends for a long while now, and the dynamics worked so well. Angel and Maria were good friends, as were he and Luke. He and Angel had never been close, and he hadn't been too enthusiastic about her relationship with Luke at first, but she'd impressed him with the way she'd handled that. She'd appreciated that he was only looking out for his buddy and had gone out of her way to show him that she, too, had Luke's best interests at heart. She'd even admitted that she didn't have a great track record with relationships and asked him to tell her if he thought she was doing something wrong. He had a lot of respect for her. Luke and Maria were both open and easy going. The four of them made a great group with lots of good conversation and easy laughs.

Angel and Luke had left a while ago to go home and get changed. They were all meeting up with the rest of their friends at the Boathouse to watch the band, and if Maria got her way, to dance the night away.

He was sitting in the kitchen waiting for her to come down so they could leave. There was a knock on the door that lead to the annex. "Come on in." He could never quite forget that Manny and the guys were over there, but he managed not to focus on it most of the time.

"Are you ready to go?"

Zack smiled. "Just as soon as she's ready."

Manny smiled back at him. "Do we need to stand down a while?"

Maria came down the stairs at that moment. "Hey. I'm not one of those girls who takes forever to get ready."

She looked amazing. Zack went to her and kissed her cheek. "No, you don't need to. You're beautiful anyway."

Maria rolled her eyes at Manny. "He's such a sweet-talker."

"He is, but he's telling the truth."

"Aww. Thank you." Maria smiled. "Or are you just as bad as him?"

Manny laughed. "No. I don't pay compliments lightly." He looked at Zack. "Then again, I guess that does make us similar after all."

Zack nodded. "Are you sure that you taking us is the way to go? I thought you were staying off the radar. We don't want to scare him away."

"It's a calculated risk. I don't want you driving yourselves. The guys are going to go out the back way. They'll be at the restaurant the whole time tonight."

Maria looked at him wide-eyed. "Has something changed?"

"No," said Manny. "You'd be taking a cab home tonight anyway so why not let me be your chauffeur?"

She smiled and seemed to accept that. Zack wasn't so sure he did. He knew Manny must have something in mind to make him change things up like this, but he wasn't telling.

~ ~ ~

Maria loved walking into the Boathouse holding Zack's hand. It seemed he was happy about it, too. He squeezed her hand and smiled at her. "How would you feel about coming to say hi to Clay and Marianne?"

She nodded nervously. "Sure. Let's jump right in at the deep end, why don't we?"

Zack raised an eyebrow.

"Clay's your boss, for starters. Not to mention the fact that he's a country music superstar. He might have blended in so well that we all forget about that most of the time, but he is. And have you forgotten who Marianne is?"

It was almost comical to watch realization dawn on his face, transforming his puzzled frown into nervous understanding. "Oh, shit! I didn't think. She's friends with your parents, isn't she?"

Maria nodded solemnly. "She's a wonderful woman. She's been so good to me over the years. She's the one who set me up to come and work for Laura."

"If it helps, I know she likes me. She hangs out with Luke and me sometimes when we fly her and Clay around."

"I don't doubt that she'll approve of you. I just don't want to put her in a difficult position. I haven't told my parents about us yet, but I can hardly ask her not to. Too late." Marianne was waving at her. She and Clay were sitting at a table over by the edge of the stage. Maria gripped Zack's hand a little tighter. "Let's go do this."

When they reached the table, Marianne got to her feet and wrapped Maria in a hug. "It's good to see you out and looking so happy."

"It's good to see you, too."

Marianne smiled at Zack. "I hear you're the one who's making our Maria so happy."

Zack nodded.

Maria felt bad for him. The poor guy was being put on the spot. He'd been so happy to tell everyone that they were together and now he was holding back because he didn't want to make life difficult for her.

"He is," she said. "He makes me very happy indeed."

Clay had gotten to his feet, too, and shook Zack's hand. "I'm glad to see the two of you have finally made it." He winked at Maria. "He's waited a long time for this."

Maria looked at Zack and he shrugged. "Clay's a good listener."

Marianne smiled. "And what do your folks have to say, Maria? Are you going to take Zack home to meet them, or are they going to come out here?"

Maria took a deep breath and looked Marianne in the eye. She couldn't lie. "I haven't actually told them about him yet."

Marianne nodded. "I did wonder."

"I know they're going to love Zack. They'll be happy for us. They won't be thrilled that we moved in together, but ..." She shrugged.

Zack put his arm around her shoulders. "It's my fault. I come with some baggage that Maria would rather put behind us before we tell her folks."

Clay pursed his lips. "I've never dug too deep into what you're hiding. I trust you. Can Maria's parents trust you?"

Zack nodded and Maria loved both men just a little bit more after that exchange. Clay was the kind of father figure any girl would love to have—once she accepted the fact that he was too old to be anything else! He looked out for the younger folk around him. To be fair, he looked out for everyone. He was just that kind of guy.

"You know all that mystery from my past?" asked Zack.

Clay nodded.

"Well, I'm hoping to have it all resolved here soon. And once it's behind us, we'll invite Maria's folks here, or we'll go there, whatever they want."

Maria rested her head against his shoulder. He was doing the best he could.

Marianne smiled at her. "I don't disapprove. I like this guy." She patted Zack's arm. "I don't know his whole story, but I do know he can be trusted. And don't worry. I don't talk to your folks very often. And I know from my experience with Laura that, as a parent, there are some things you're better off not knowing about until they're resolved."

Maria breathed a sigh of relief. "Thank you. I'm not trying to deceive them or anything. I just don't want them to worry."

"I know. I understand. But if I can do anything to help you, you let me know, okay?"

Maria gave her another hug. "I will. Thank you."

Clay smiled at Zack. "The same thing goes for you, son. I'd love to help, if there's anything I can do."

"Thanks," said Zack. "I need to do this for myself, but I appreciate the offer."

"Hey guys." They all turned as Chase and Eddie, the guys in the band came to join them. Maria smiled, remembering how she used to wonder what might be going on between Zack and April. She was glad to know that his connection was actually with her fiancé, Eddie.

"How's it going?" Zack smiled at them

"Great, thanks." Eddie smiled at Maria. "I hear things are going well for the two of you."

Maria nodded happily, but she didn't miss the inquiring look he gave Zack.

"Mind if I join you for a couple of numbers tonight?" Clay asked Chase.

"Not at all, we're here to ask if you want to."

Maria loved that Clay was so down to earth. He was probably the biggest name in country music, but he'd befriended the guys in the local band, and sometimes, when it wasn't too busy, he got up and sang with them.

"We'll leave you to it," said Zack.

Maria hugged Marianne one more time, and then they made their way over to one of the long tables where Angel and Luke were sitting with Roxy and Colt.

Roxy beamed at them. "I still can't get over how awesome it is to see you two together."

Maria laughed. "Thank you. I kind of feel the same way."

Roxy made a face. "But I am a little offended that you didn't invite me over this afternoon, especially since I was kind of instrumental in getting you together. I hope the four of you aren't going to start leaving the rest of us out now that you're all coupled up."

"Of course not," began Angel, looking worried.

Maria just laughed. "Maybe we will, just as an incentive for you to get yourself a guy, too."

Roxy rolled her eyes at Colt. "No offense or anything, Colt, but I don't know anyone I would want to couple up with."

"That's so not true!" said Maria.

Colt laughed. "Sorry, Rox, but we all know that you like Logan."

She made a face. "I'm talking about being a couple, not the down and dirty kind of physical coupling, which is all he thinks women are good for."

Colt nodded. "Yeah, you've got a point there."

"Anyway. You're going to be left out, too. The only date you've been on in months was with what's-her-face, Nadia's crony."

Colt blew out a sigh but didn't comment.

"But we're hoping to change that, aren't we girls?" asked Maria.

Colt ran a hand through his hair and gave her a worried look. "What are you talking about?"

She grinned at him. "I told you Amber and Jade were coming for dinner with us the other night. Well, they did, and we invited them to come along tonight, too. They said they would."

"Is Austin coming?" asked Zack.

"Yeah, he is," said Luke. "I saw him this afternoon."

Roxy made a face. "Tell me he's not bringing Nadia?"

"Aww, don't be like that," said Maria. "We have to be nice to her for his sake."

"You're just too nice," said Roxy. "I'd rather tell her where to shove it and then get Austin interested in someone else."

"I think he might already be interested in someone else." Maria turned to look at Zack, wondering what made him think that.

"I ran into him and those two girls in here one morning. If I had to guess, I'd say that Logan had it right and that Austin likes the blonde sister."

"Wow." Maria didn't know what to make of that. She didn't care for Nadia, but she didn't see Austin as the kind of guy who would cheat.

Luke frowned, seemingly thinking the same as Maria. "Then it's time he broke up with Nadia. I don't like her, but that's not fair to her."

They were all quiet for a few moments until Logan appeared. He looked around the table and laughed. "Damn, guys. I know you all need me to be the life and soul of the party, but could you at least look like you're having a little fun? Especially you two." He smiled at Maria and Zack. "You know I'm not big on the mushy stuff and I don't get why two such good-looking people would want to take themselves off the market, but as long as you're happy, I'm happy for you."

Maria had to laugh. "Thanks. I think."

Logan waggled his eyebrows at her. "You can always call me if ever you change your mind."

"I won't." She took hold of Zack's hand and squeezed it, hoping to let him know that she wouldn't *ever* change her mind.

"Why are we all so serious, anyway?" asked Logan.

"What do you know about Lenny's granddaughters?" asked Zack.

Logan shrugged. "I know all I need to know. They're off limits. Lenny would skin me alive if I made a move on either of them."

Maria laughed. "Lenny's a sweetie. Why would you say that?"

"Because I grew up living around the corner from her, and as you can maybe imagine, I was a little terror. She didn't take any of my shit back then—she dragged me home by the ear more than a few times. I'm not going to risk incurring her wrath now." He smiled, and Maria could tell he was softer than he made out. There was more to him than his women chasing and storytelling ways. "She has to take it easy after her heart attack."

Colt smiled at him. "You were a little terror, but Lenny always had a soft spot for you. And you still have one for her."

Logan shrugged. "Yeah, okay, I do. Lenny's awesome. So, there's no way I'd go anywhere near one of her granddaughters." He looked at Zack. "Why do you want to know? And should you really be asking in front of Maria?"

Zack scowled at him. "You wanted to know why we were all looking thoughtful when you arrived. It's because we were talking about Austin."

"Ah." Logan was unperturbed by Zack's irritation with him. "Yeah. I'd say Nadia will have to look out. Austin seemed smitten with the blonde one."

"Amber." Maria shook her head. "Why do you have to describe women by their hair color instead of calling them by name?"

Logan grinned. "I have no memory for names, so I have to use the details that stick with me. You, for example, for the first few months I knew you, you were great set, great ass." He turned to Angel. "You were leggy blonde, pouty smile. And you …" He turned to Roxy, but his smile faded in the face of the withering look she gave him. "You are about to tell me to shut up, right? And I think you might have a point. Want to come and help me get a round in, Colt?"

Colt got to his feet and the two of them went to the bar.

Roxy shook her head. "He really is an asshole!"

"And it only bothers you so much because you like him," said Angel.

Roxy shrugged but didn't comment.

It was going on midnight by the time they came out of the restaurant. Zack had his arm around the girl's shoulders. Morales slid down a little lower in his seat. He doubted they'd see him. Zack seemed to be letting his guard down. He probably thought he was safe since Alvarado was waiting in the truck to take them home. He might be safe for now, but he wouldn't be for much longer. Morales was growing impatient.

That wasn't his nature. He was a firm believer that revenge was a dish best served cold. But his vengeance for his brother's death had been left to cool for so long that his blood now ran with ice cold fury through his veins. Zack was only a few years younger than Alejandro. Why should he get to live, to take a woman, when Alejandro lay dead in the ground?

He banged his fist against his thigh. He shouldn't. That was the simple answer. Zack Aguila had taken his brother's life and it was time for him to pay with his own.

Chapter Seventeen

Zack sat at the island in the kitchen watching Maria gather her things up as she got ready for work. "I wish you didn't have to go."

She came to him and landed a kiss on his lips. "So do I, but this is my life. I have to get up and go to work every day. I don't get to sit around drinking coffee most of the time and jet off to exotic locations on the few days I do have to do anything."

He made a face at her. "You make me sound like a lazy bum."

"Aww, I don't mean to. I guess I just have a case of the Monday morning blues. I would have loved to sleep in a little longer." She ran her hand up his thigh. "To have had some more time in bed with you. I wish I could spend the day here with you. We only have another week before you have to take Clay back to Nashville—and who knows how long you'll be gone for."

"I know. I'm sorry. I wish you could stay home with me."

She shrugged. "So, do I. But that's not my reality. I have to go to work to pay my rent."

He caught her eye and raised an eyebrow.

She blew out a sigh. "Okay. You know what I mean. Just because we're living here and I'm living off you …"

He closed his arms around her. "You're not living off me. Take that back. You're still paying your rent—though maybe we should talk about that. About whether we really want to keep your house on."

She looked up into his eyes. "I thought we were going to wait to see what happened first. I thought us staying here was only temporary."

He rested his forehead against hers. "So did I. I don't know what I'm saying. All I know is what I'm feeling. I said this was only temporary, but I don't want it to be. I know you like it here now that you're used to it. Why can't we make this our home? I told you you're not getting rid of me. So, why should you keep your old place? Why should I keep mine?"

She stepped back and pursed her lips. "That's a lot of questions and I can't even think about the answers right now." She looked up at the clock on the wall. "I need to get going or I'm going to be late for work."

"I know. I'm sorry. It's the wrong time to bring it up, but can we talk about it? Tonight, maybe?"

"Okay. I'll see you when I get home."

He cupped his hands around the sides of her neck and kissed her. It was a low blow; he knew that move turned her on. She relaxed against him and kissed him back for a few moments before she came to her senses and stepped away, narrowing her eyes at him. "You weren't kidding when you said you can be very persuasive, were you?"

He smiled. "No. I love you, my little peanut, why wouldn't I try to persuade you to go all in with me, to give up your place and make this our home?"

She smiled back at him. "I'm not complaining about your intentions. I love it. I love you. It's just that your timing isn't wonderful. I really have to go or I'm going to be late."

"Sorry. You go. One of the guys already went out to the car on the back lane. They'll follow you once you hit West Shore Drive."

She made a face. "I know that's how it's supposed to work, but I've never once spotted them following me."

He smiled. "That's how it's supposed to be."

After she'd left, he went through to the annex to find Manny.

"Morning." Manny held up his mug of coffee. "You want one?"

"No, thanks. What I want is talk to you about how we can hurry this up. I'm going crazy here."

"I know. I get it. I'd like to see if we can't move things along faster, too. I'm going to have to go back to the office at some point. I gave myself a month, in the hope that that would be more than enough, but time's running out."

"I know you can't stay here babysitting me forever." Zack gave him a rueful smile. "And much as I love you, I don't want you here. I want to get on with my life. I want to set up home with Maria—in this house or another one if that's what she wants. This place is perfect for now, but I don't know that she'll want to stay on here."

Manny gave him a puzzled look. "I'd have thought a young girl like that would be thrilled to move into a place like this with her rich, handsome boyfriend. It's like a Cinderella story."

Zack laughed. "She's not interested in being a Cinderella. She'd rather be Super Girl. She doesn't need me to swoop in and be her hero or her prince. She's perfectly capable of kicking ass herself."

Manny chuckled. "True. That's why I like her so much."

"And it's partly why I love her. There's so much about her to love."

Manny nodded. "I think the two of you have a long and happy future ahead of you."

"I hope so, but first we have to keep me alive and the way to do that is take Morales down."

"Yeah. I've been setting things up a little differently than we discussed."

"I know. That's why you went everywhere with us this weekend, right?"

"Yep. I figured Morales was taking his time while he works out how easy a target you're going to be. I decided to show our hand—at least in part. If he's watching, and I'll put money on the fact that he is, then he now knows that I'm here, and that I go most places with you—whenever you and Maria are together. So now he knows that you're going to be easier to get to when you're on your own."

Zack smiled. "Thanks."

Manny smiled back at him. "I know how important she is to you."

"Yeah. I want him to come after me when I'm alone. Keep her as far out of it as possible."

"Exactly. So, now I want you to come up with something that you do every day, at the same time. Alone."

Zack thought about it. "I could join the gym?"

Manny nodded. "Do you know the place? Know the layout?"

Zack shook his head.

"Then let's go."

Zack frowned. "You want him to see the two of us out together?"

"Nope. You're driving. I'll just make myself comfortable on the back seat. I can scope out the exterior while you go in and sign up."

~ ~ ~

"I want to close up a little earlier tonight," said Laura.

"I'm not going to argue with you about that," said Maria with a smile. It'd been a long week and she was ready for it to be over. It was Thursday and an early finish would get them a little bit closer to weekend. "You've been back here working on your designs all week without a break, and I've been busy out front."

"I know. I'm sure you won't mind getting home to Zack early."

"And I'm sure you won't mind getting home to Smoke. I bet you love having him home for this long, don't you?"

Laura laughed. "I do, but at the same time you know I have a perfectly good workshop out in the orchard at home—but I've been in here all week."

"Oh. I didn't realize. I thought you were coming in here ..." She stopped herself.

"Well, I didn't want to leave you in here by yourself at the moment. I don't like that idea. But, yeah. It can be hard to get anything done with Smoke home. He thinks since he's off, I should be, too."

"Zack's the same way. He makes it hard to come out to work in the morning." She smiled. "Very hard."

"It's not easy being married to a pilot, I have to warn you. It's all or nothing. You miss them when they're gone, and you have to find the balance when they're home."

Maria didn't say anything, but she could feel the color in her cheeks.

Laura gave her a knowing smile. "I know, I know. Who said anything about you and Zack getting married, right? But that's where it's going. I know it is."

Maria nodded. "I'd be a liar if I said I didn't like that idea."

"And I wouldn't believe you if you did. I just hope all this crazy business with that man who's after him is over soon."

"I can't wait. I know I should probably feel scared and be more careful than I am, but I can't. I can't make the threat feel real. All I feel is angry and irritated. I want it all to be over. I want us to be free to move forward."

"Surely something has to happen soon. Even if he doesn't make a move, I hope those detectives or whatever they are, are trying to track him down, too."

"I think they're more focused on drawing him out. They seem to think the only way they'll ever find him is by waiting for him to attack Zack."

Laura blew out a sigh. "I hope Zack's going to be ready when he does."

"He will be. That's another reason I can't get too worked up about it. He's so confident that all it's going to take is Morales coming after him, and he'll be able to handle it—and of course, Manny and his men won't be too far away."

"I admire his confidence. I just hope he's right."

Maria nodded. She did too. She just couldn't allow herself to think that there was any other possible outcome.

Laura looked out through the front window as someone walked by. "I still can't believe that there's some guy out there keeping a look out for you and we've never spotted him."

Maria had to laugh. "Sometimes, I wonder if they just tell me that he's there to make me feel better."

Laura laughed with her. "He's good at staying out of sight, but I can't believe for a minute that Zack would let you even come to work if there wasn't someone close by to step in if you need it."

"I know … oh, is that Emma?"

Laura smiled. "It is. We're having a girls' night over here tonight. She said she might come by if she arrived early."

The doorbell buzzed when Emma opened the door and came in with a big smile. "Hello, ladies. How are you?"

"I'm good, thanks, Em," said Laura. "We're going to close up in a few minutes."

"Take your time. I know I'm early. I thought I'd rather come and see all your pretty, shiny things than go and sit in the café by myself." She smiled at Maria. "And how are you? Are you coming tonight?"

Maria shook her head.

"No. She has the lovely Zack at home waiting for her," said Laura.

"Oh, of course. He is lovely, too." Emma grinned at Maria. "He's yummy. I have to tell you I have a thing for the tall, dark, handsome ones."

Laura laughed. "She's not joking either. She's had a crush on Missy's brother, Chance, for what, twenty years?"

Emma nodded happily. "He's lovely, too. But I only like to look. Jack's the only one for me."

Maria smiled at her. She liked Emma. "Does Jack have little Isabel tonight?"

"He does. It's so sweet; he and Pete have her and little baby, Noah."

They all looked up when the door opened again, and Missy came in. "Hi, girls. Sorry, I didn't get to your place in time to ride over here with you, Em, but I got Scotty to drop me off so I can have a drink and ride back with you."

Laura shook her head. "It's still hard to believe that Scott's driving these days."

"Isn't it?" asked Emma. "And even scarier for me to think that before I know it, Isabel will be, too."

Missy laughed. "The time goes by fast, but you've got a little while yet, Em." She turned to Maria. "Are you coming tonight?"

"No, not this time."

Missy nodded. "It's funny how we're all at different stages, but we all still get along so well. I've got Scott who's almost grown. Em's got little Isabel. Laura … I still don't know about you. I'm sure you always said never when it came to babies, but now it's, never say never."

Maria watched Laura's reaction. She, too, had started to wonder if she and Smoke might announce they were pregnant one day.

Missy turned back to Maria. "And you. You and Zack are just getting started, but I think you're on the same path we all are. I hope the two of you have babies; they'd be gorgeous. I mean you're both so good-looking. You couldn't produce anything but beautiful children."

Maria laughed. "Like you said, we're just getting started. That's a long way off."

Missy smiled. "Maybe, but you didn't tell me not to be ridiculous, did you?"

Maria felt the color in her cheeks. Missy was right. She hadn't told her not to be silly, because she herself didn't think it was silly; in fact, she loved the idea.

"Okay," said Laura. "I think we need to move this over to the café. Why don't the two of you meet me there and I'll lock up and come around."

"I can lock up," said Maria. "You go out the front with them and I'll lock up inside and then let myself out the back."

"No freaking way." Laura shook her head adamantly.

"Why's that?" asked Missy.

Laura frowned. "Because I don't like leaving Maria to go out there by herself."

Missy nodded. "Then we'll all go out the back. We can see Maria safe into her car and then walk round to the café together. Will we go past the back of Holly's store on the way?"

Laura nodded. "Yeah. We can see if she's still there."

Maria wanted to tell them she was fine, but she loved the way they all looked out for each other—and that she was included in that.

When they were all outside, Laura locked the door and they walked Maria over to her car. All the little hairs on the back of Maria's neck stood up at the thought that they were being watched. They were; but only by Manny's guy who'd been watching her every day for weeks now.

She opened her car door and got in. "Thanks, ladies. I hope you have a great evening."

Missy frowned at her. "I thought we were just being overly cautious coming out here with you. Why do you need that?"

Maria didn't need to follow her gaze to know that she'd spotted the baseball bat she kept behind her seat. She smiled and tried to make light of it. "Hopefully, I don't. But what's that saying? It's better to have it and not need it than need it and not have it, right?"

Missy wrinkled her nose. "If you say so. Are you sure you're okay?"

Maria gave her a reassuring smile. "I'm fine, really. Right, Laura?"

Laura nodded. "So you keep telling me."

They all turned at the sound of car tires screeching as they pulled away.

Emma shuddered. "Eesh. This is freaking me out. Do you want us to follow you home, make sure you get there okay?"

Maria smiled. "No, honestly. I'm fine." She wanted to tell them that there would be someone following her home and he'd probably be of more help if she needed him.

"You go," said Laura. "I want to see you drive away before we leave."

"Okay. See you tomorrow." She closed the door and started the engine, then watched them all waving in the rearview mirror as she pulled away. When she pulled out onto East Shore, she checked the mirror a few more times, but if there was anyone following her—good guy or bad guy—she didn't see them.

When she got back to the house, she waited impatiently while the gate swung open, grateful that she had her own remote and didn't have to open her window and press the buzzer. She was on edge. She'd managed to not allow herself to think too deeply about Morales and what might happen, but something about the way the girls had acted tonight had burst her bubble. She was scared.

She drove into the garage and closed the door behind her before she got out of her car. Then ran for the door that led into the kitchen.

Zack was standing there at the island, pouring them each a glass of wine. She went straight to him and closed her arms around him.

"Hey!" He wrapped her up in a hug. "Are you okay? What's wrong?"

She buried her face in his chest. "I'm scared, Zack. It hit me tonight that he might really get you. He could hurt you—he could kill you. I can't stand it. Why don't we leave? You've done okay all this time by hiding and moving on. We should do that. I don't want you to let him find you."

He hugged her to his chest and dropped a kiss on top of her head. "It's okay, peanut. It's all going to be okay."

"You don't know that. You can't know that. We should run while we can."

He tucked his fingers under her chin and made her look up into his eyes. "I do know that. It's going to be over soon. I saw him today when I came out of the gym. He wanted me to see him. He's letting me know he's going to make his move soon."

Her blood ran cold. "Then we need to leave. Now!"

"No. If we run now, we'll be running forever. It needs to end."

"But Zack ..."

"It's going to be okay. I told you. I love you. You're stuck with me forever."

She had to blink away tears as she buried her face in his chest. "Forever had better be a really, really long time."

Chapter Eighteen

Maria didn't want to go to work the next morning. She wanted to stay with Zack. She had a horrible sense of foreboding.

He took hold of her hand as they sat at the island eating breakfast. "It's going to be okay."

She shook her head. "You can't know that. You have to go back to Nashville on Monday and then what? Will he know where you've gone? Will he follow you? Will he decide that since you're not here he may as well come after me?"

"No!" Zack shook his head. "I talked to Clay yesterday. I'm not going. I was going to surprise you, but you need to know, I'm not going anywhere till this is over."

"But you have to. It's your job."

"It is, but I have to do what's best for everyone. I explained things to Clay, and I talked to Luke. One of Smoke's pilots is going to stand in for me."

Maria blew out a sigh. "Okay. Good. I'm glad they're all taken care of. I still think we should just pack up and leave though."

He squeezed her hand. "Not now. We're almost there. He's going to make his move. I can feel it."

"I can too! That's why I'm saying we should go, before he gets the chance."

"I'll be okay. I promise you. You need to get ready. You're going to be late."

"I don't want to go."

"You'll feel better if you do. It'll take your mind off it."

"I don't want to take my mind off it! I don't want to think about anything except keeping the man I love alive."

He smiled. "Don't worry … I'm kind of focused on that, too. So's Manny."

She frowned. "What are you going to do today?"

"I'm going to go to the gym this morning, same as I have every day this week."

Maria scowled. "So that you're in the same place at the same time so that he can find you easily and try to kill you, right?"

"Yes. So that we can get this over with. I know you think it's crazy, but at least this way, we're in control of the circumstances."

She nodded sadly. "I know. I know all the logic. I get it. But I just can't think logically right now. I love you too much to lose you."

"And I love you too much to let anything take me away from you. We're forever you and me, peanut. And dealing with Morales is the beginning of our forever, not the end."

She nodded. "Okay, but I want you to call me, like every half hour or something."

He smiled. "I'll call you before I go to the gym, and I'll call you when I get back."

"What if you don't get back? What if something happens to you?"

He squeezed her hand. "I'll call you."

She slid down from the stool. "You'd better. I'm going to go to work, but only because if I stay here, I'm going to drive us both nuts."

"Just try to have a normal day. There's no saying that today is going to be it."

"There is. I know it. I can feel it."

He walked her to her car in the garage and held her close before she got in. "It's going to be okay. I promise. I love you too much to let anything happen. I need to do this, Maria. I need to end it."

She had to blink back tears. "I love you, Zack. If you change your mind just call me. We can leave town, start over somewhere else. I'd rather do that, live life on the move with you than ... than ..."

"We won't have to. I'll see you tonight."

~ ~ ~

After she'd left, Zack went back into the kitchen. He hated to make her worry, but he knew it all had to go down this way. He'd promised her it would all be okay, and he intended to do everything in his power to make sure that it would, but there was a niggling fear that maybe he wouldn't be able to do enough. What if Morales surprised him? He and Manny had gone over all the scenarios they could come up with. Any place that Morales might come after him, they had a plan. Zack wasn't a fighter by nature, but after his experience at the hands of Morales and his brother, he'd taken all kinds of self-defense and martial arts classes. He knew enough, he hoped, to at least keep Morales at bay until Manny arrived to help. And Manny would never be too far away.

In the early days, he'd been afraid that Morales might just shoot him—pick him off from a couple hundred yards away with a rifle. But the FBI profilers had assured him that that was highly unlikely. Morales wanted revenge. This was personal. Zack wasn't a stranger to him; he'd been Morales' victim—his hostage—for weeks. His profile said that Morales was most likely to attack with a knife. Zack shuddered at the sure knowledge that that bastard would want to look him in the eyes and see his pain while he twisted a knife in his guts and watched him die.

He jumped when Manny came through from the annex. "Jesus!"

"What's up?"

Zack shook his head. "I'm just psyching myself out, I guess. Maria was upset this morning and she set me thinking and …" He shrugged. "She has a feeling that today's the day, and I think she's right."

Manny nodded solemnly. "That makes three of us. After all this time, I thought it would still come as a surprise—take us unaware—but I'd bet my life on it being today."

Zack gave him a rueful smile. "You don't need to do that … we'll just bet mine."

"It's not much of a gamble, Zack. We've got this. I'll be with you the whole time."

"I know. I'm feeling a weird kind of calm. Either I'm just so ready for it to be over that I'm okay with it," he gave a small laugh, "or some part of me knows I'm going to die."

Manny scowled at him. "Not going to happen. Not on my watch."

~ ~ ~

Maria couldn't focus at work. All she could think about was Zack and Morales and what might happen and whether Zack would still be okay by the time she got home—she couldn't let her mind go near the question of if he'd still be alive! She needed to have as much faith in him and Manny as he did.

Laura came out from her workshop in the back and gave her an odd look when she noticed that Maria was still polishing the same ring she'd been polishing twenty minutes ago. "Are you sure you want to be here today?"

Maria blew out a sigh. "I'm sure that I don't, but it's probably better that I am."

"What's up? I knew there was something wrong since you got here."

"It feels like today's the day. I think that man is going to find Zack today and when he does … I … I …" She burst into tears.

Laura came and put an arm around her shoulders. "Hey. Come on. Zack's going to be fine. He's smart and he's strong and he has Manny with him. I know it must be hard, but look on the bright side. You're so good at that. Hopefully by tonight, the guy will be behind bars and you and Zack will finally be able to breathe easy. It'll all be over. You can take some time off if you want. The two of you can go away together."

Maria nodded and sniffed. "You're right. I'm sorry. I need to think about how good it will be after this is over. I can't let myself focus on how shitty it feels right now. How scared I am. Sorry. I'm a mess. It just got to me. I'll pull myself together. I'm better than this."

Laura smiled at her. "You're allowed to let it all out. Cry … admit you're scared. You've dealt with all this in a way I don't think many people could. You've stayed strong, you've been upbeat, it was bound to get to you at some point. Don't be hard on yourself, *chica*. You're doing great, don't start telling yourself otherwise."

Maria wiped her face and nodded. "Thanks, Laura. I feel like a pressure cooker and I just needed to let a bit of steam out."

"I'm glad you could. I've been worried about you. You've been putting on a brave face, but I know it must be killing you inside. It's killing me, and I don't know Zack that well. I'm worried for him, though. You really don't want to go home?"

"No. I might go when he calls to say he's back. That'll mean it's not today, and I'll be so relieved."

"Maybe he'll call to say it's all over?"

Maria smiled. "Yeah. Maybe. That's a bright side I can hope for."

~ ~ ~

Zack finished his workout and showered. His mind was racing. If his gut was right, then he was within minutes of finally coming face to face with Morales again. It would be the first time in over ten years, and one way or another, it would probably be the last.

He toweled himself off and got dressed. He had to smile as he put on clean underwear—it was better to be wearing clean underwear if you were going to die. He blew out a sigh. It wasn't a joking matter. There was a very real possibility that he might die today. Adrenaline surged through his veins. No. No way in hell was he going to let that bastard take him down. Not now. Not when he and Maria were all set to begin their life together. Morales had already stolen too much from him. There was no way Zack would let him take away his life and his love.

When he was dressed, he picked up his bag and made his way to the back door. He stopped before he reached it to send Manny a quick text.

I'm on the way out. Any signs?

Manny's reply came almost instantly.

Nothing.

Zack nodded. It wasn't as though he expected Morales to be standing in the middle of the parking lot brandishing a machete. He tapped out a reply wondering why he was bothering. Manny was hardly going to be thinking that he might have changed his mind and decided to go for a beer instead.

Ok. I'm going straight to the old road.

It appeared that Manny felt the need to state the obvious, too.

I'll be there.

"You'd better be," Zack murmured under his breath as he pushed the door open.

As he drove out the old road that followed the river, his heart was racing. He knew how to lower his heart rate by controlling his breathing, but he wasn't capable of it today. Maybe adrenaline interfered with that process—and there was plenty of adrenaline flowing.

He reached the pullout and parked the truck in the same spot he'd used all week. There were no other vehicles out here. That was good. At least, he hoped it was good. It meant there was no one else around. At least no unknown others, but did it mean that Morales had left his vehicle somewhere else and already positioned himself somewhere along the path? Did it mean that Manny had parked somewhere so far away that he wouldn't be able to come to his aid fast enough if Morales did make his move?

Zack made himself breathe slowly and pulled his heel up to his ass to stretch his quads. He made himself stretch slowly and calmly and took advantage of the time to check out every direction he could. If there was another living soul out here, he couldn't spot them.

When he couldn't put it off any longer, he started to jog down the path, exactly as he'd done every day this week.

~ ~ ~

Maria pulled into the parking lot at the gym. Zack's truck wasn't there. She knew he wouldn't want her to be here, but she just couldn't sit at work and do nothing. Laura had told her to go home, but she couldn't go and sit there, either. She hated not knowing what was going on—if he was okay?

"No." She said it out loud, and so forcefully that she surprised herself. If his truck wasn't here, then he'd gone for his run. He went down the old road out by the river. She could take a drive by. He might be mad if he spotted her, but she might be able to stay out of the way. She looked around, remembering that one of Manny's guys would be watching her right now.

For the first time, she called the number she had for him.

"Ma'am?" he answered.

"For God's sake would you call me Maria?"

"Yes, ma'... Maria. What are you doing?"

"I'm going out to the old road."

"I can't allow you to do that. You need to go home."

"I can't go home! I need to go. I might be able to help."

"With all due respect, ma'... Maria, Special Agent Alvarado is not going to want you anywhere near. You could put Zack in danger by being there."

"I won't. And did you ever think you could put him in danger by not being there?"

The line was quiet for a moment.

"Exactly," said Maria and hung up. She pulled out of the parking lot and looked around, wondering if she might be able to spot him coming after her. She still couldn't.

When she reached the pullout, she felt a sense of relief when she saw Zack's truck parked there. She got out and looked around. There were no other vehicles anywhere near. She walked a little way down the road. Nothing. So, Morales mustn't be here. She frowned. There was no sign of Manny either. Maybe they both left their vehicles somewhere else? She felt stupid. Of course, they would. They both knew how to do this. She, on the other hand, was bumbling around in the middle of it all, possibly about to screw everything up. She finally understood that this was the wrong move and started back toward her car. She needed to get out of here.

The pathway, where she knew Zack took his run, ran parallel to the road, dropping down toward the river, whose path it followed all the way back to the lake. She heard someone coming; it was Zack! And then she saw him. Manny had shown her a photo of Morales when he first arrived. She'd been surprised that he looked so normal. She wouldn't have picked him out of a line-up as someone who looked like a criminal. Right now, perched on the embankment above the path, he looked like an evil demon waiting to pounce.

"Zack!" She called his name to warn him, without stopping to think.

Zack's expression was shocked when he saw her, and then stunned when Morales jumped down from the embankment and landed on Zack taking them both to the ground.

"Oh, my God!" Maria looked around. Where was Manny? Where were the two agents? She couldn't see anyone. She ran back to her car. All she could think of was the baseball bat under her seat. Maybe she could jump down on Morales and get him with one good hit.

By the time she'd grabbed the bat and run back to her vantage point above the path, what she saw paralyzed her.

Zack and Morales were trading blows—and Zack was covered in blood. Where the fuck was Manny?

"Drop your weapon." There he was.

He had a gun trained on Morales, but there was no way he could take a shot while he and Zack were bearhugging each other to better beat the crap out of each other.

"Zack!" Manny obviously wanted him to move away, but Morales wasn't letting go and Zack didn't seem to want to stop punching.

Maria watched in horror as Morales locked his arm around Zack's neck. He was going to strangle him! Manny couldn't shoot him—there was too much risk of him hitting Zack. She looked down at her baseball bat and started to slide her way down the embankment. Manny could see her, but Zack and Morales had their backs to her.

She slid a little way and hoped she wouldn't fall all the way down. A strong hand reached out and grabbed her and she had to bite back a scream. It was the other agent—why had she never learned their names?

He gestured for her to get back and then reached for her bat. She handed it over willingly. Even if she'd been able to get down there without Morales seeing her coming. She doubted she would have been able to hit him hard enough to knock him out.

She watched as the agent slid down the rest of the way and landed just behind Morales. Manny had kept talking loudly the whole time, commanding Morales to drop his weapon—though if he still had a weapon, Maria couldn't see it. He seemed intent on choking Zack to death, since stabbing him hadn't worked.

He must have heard the agent land behind him. He turned at the sound, and in doing so, loosened his grip on Zack. Zack twisted out of his stranglehold and rolled away, just as Maria's bat made contact with the side of Morales' head.

Maria cringed and covered her eyes as he went down. Then she scrambled to her feet and slid the rest of the way down the embankment. Manny reached Zack just before she did, but she pushed him out of the way and hauled Zack up in her arms.

"Are you okay? What did he do? Where did he stab you?"

Zack held a hand over the bloodstain just above his right hip.

Maria looked at Manny. "Can you get him an ambulance? Quick!"

Manny nodded and jerked his chin at the third agent who was talking on his phone several yards away.

"He was here, too?" She asked indignantly. "Why did none of you stop him?"

"We didn't know where he was until you shouted. Then he was on Zack and there was nothing we could do without putting Zack at risk."

Zack smiled up her. "Did you bring a towel rail?"

She laughed, aware that it might sound a little hysterical. She was just so relieved.

"A baseball bat." The other agent smiled at them, even as he was rolling Morales onto his stomach and cuffing his hands behind his back. "I want to be mad at you ma'am, Maria, but you brought the perfect weapon."

She smiled at him and then looked at Manny, realizing for the first time that he might be madder than hell at her.

He gave her a wry smile. "It all worked out."

She kissed Zack's forehead. "Does this mean it's all over?" He smiled up at her. "It does. I told you it would be."

She couldn't hold back the tears, it was relief—that was all, but the tears flowed freely down over her cheeks. She lifted his shirt up to see how bad it was.

"It's not bad," said Manny.

Zack looked at him. "That's easy for you to say."

Manny laughed. "True, but it's not life-threatening. How about that?"

Zack smiled. "I'll take it."

"It's going to need stitches," said Maria. "Lots of them."

Zack smiled at her. "That's a small price to pay."

Manny got to his feet and offered Zack his hand. "Come on. Let's get you back up to the road. They'll want to take you to the hospital to get that taken care of."

Zack put one arm around Manny's shoulders and the other around Maria and they made their way back up to the road.

Manny smiled at Zack. "You were right when you said she's super girl. She doesn't need you to be her hero, but I think she just became yours."

Zack smiled at her. "She's always been my hero."

Maria's eyes filled with tears again. "And you'll always be mine."

Epilogue

"It was good of Doctor Morgan to see you on a Saturday," said Maria as they walked back to her car.

Zack smiled at her. "Michael's a good guy. I don't know him as well as some of the others, but he's the kind who'll go out of his way to help."

"What did he say about the stitches?"

"He wants me to come back on Tuesday to have them taken out."

Maria nodded. "I think I'll ask Laura if she minds if I take next week off as well."

"That'd be great." He could hardly tell her that he'd already talked to Laura about that. He was hoping that they were going to be far too busy for Maria to go into work.

He rolled his eyes at her when they reached her car and she held the passenger door open for him. "I'm not an invalid. I could have driven us here."

She laughed. "I know, but I need to feel like I'm taking care of you."

He dropped a kiss on her lips before he got in. When she came around to the driver's side, he gave her a wry smile. "Do you still feel like you need that?" He jerked his head toward the back seat where her baseball bat was sitting.

She laughed. "You just never know."

"I guess not. But I believe that our days of needing it are behind us."

She reached over and squeezed his hand. "I do, too, but after spending all that time knowing he was out there, watching, I don't think I'll ever be able to get too complacent."

"Yeah." He was relieved that Morales was now in federal custody and from what Manny had told him, he wouldn't ever be coming back. Manny said there were so many charges against him, in so many countries, that even if he wanted to make a deal, there was no way he'd ever walk free.

"What do you want to do this afternoon?" she asked as they drove through town. "Should we stop at the store?"

"No. I think we have enough at home." He smiled. There was so much more waiting at home for her than she imagined. He couldn't wait to get there.

She slowed the car as they approached the gate and then stopped. It stood wide open. She turned to him with wide eyes. "You don't think …?"

"No. I don't." He reassured her. "We need to get used to the idea that he's not coming back."

She pulled forward slowly and then stopped again to reach in the back for her bat.

Zack had to laugh. "You're not going to need it."

"How can you be sure?"

"Luke said he and Angel might stop by this afternoon. I told him the code. He probably forgot to close it after them." He hoped that would set her mind at ease. It wasn't a lie—it just wasn't the whole truth.

She pulled forward again, but he could tell she was still cautious by the way she drove slowly, peering through the windshield.

As they got closer to the house, her expression changed. There was no one hiding in wait for them; instead, there were at least a dozen vehicles parked outside.

She turned to him with a frown. "What the ...?"

He had to laugh at her expression. "Sorry. I wanted to surprise you. I invited a few people over. You've been so busy playing nurse to me all week. You only got a break when Luke took me out last night. You haven't been out at all. And we never invited people over for a housewarming, so I thought we could kill two birds with one stone."

"Why didn't you tell me? I would have made sure the place was nice ... gotten food and drink in and ..." She made a face. "I feel like a bad host now."

He reached over and tangled his fingers in her hair. "That's exactly why I didn't tell you. I knew you'd work your ass off to get everything ready, and that's not what this is about. It's all taken care of. There's food and drink—and that's not what people are here for anyway."

She pursed her lips. "Still, I wish you'd told me."

"I wanted to surprise you."

He could see the struggle on her face for a few moments but, as he'd known she would, she let it go and laughed. "Well, you've definitely done that."

"Good." He managed to stop himself from telling her that this was just the first of the surprises he had in store.

They got out of the car and he took hold of her hand and led her around the side of the house.

She stopped dead when she saw how many people were out there on the lawn. There was a long table laid out with sandwiches and hors d'oeuvres and a bar set up on the patio, just like he'd wanted.

She shook her head in disbelief and looked up at him.

"Is it okay?"

She laughed. "Okay? It's amazing! You're in charge of all our parties in the future."

He smiled and hugged her into his side. "I can do that. And I've been meaning to ask you. Do you want to hold all our parties here?"

She raised an eyebrow at him.

"I mean, does this place feel like home to you now? Do you want to stay here?"

She drew in a deep breath and blew it out, then nodded slowly. "Yes. Yes, I do. We've been through so much already, and this place kept us safe through it. It feels like our sanctuary. I know I wasn't sure at first, but I can't imagine leaving it to live somewhere else now."

He landed a kiss on her lips as relief swept through him. She'd put the way he felt about this house into words better than he could have. "Neither can I. For the first time in my adult life, I feel like I found home."

She rested her head against his shoulder with a smile, and he wanted to tell her that it was only home because he shared it with her, but he didn't get the chance.

"Look everyone. They're here!"

All heads turned in their direction and he gripped Maria's hand tightly and led her over to the lawn where a sea of smiling faces waited for them.

~ ~ ~

Maria struggled to take it all in. There were so many people. Angel and Luke stood on the patio with Roxy, Colt, Austin, and Logan.

Smoke leaned in the doorway that led out from the kitchen. He had his arm around Laura and Holly and Pete stood with them.

April and Eddie were sitting at the patio table with Kenzie and Chase and an older man she didn't recognize.

Even Clay was there, smiling at her. She smiled back and then saw Marianne standing beside him. Marianne gave her a reassuring smile and jerked her head to her left. Maria looked to see what she was trying to tell her, and her mouth fell open when she saw her parents standing there.

She squeezed Zack's hand tight. "What … how …"

He smiled down at her. "You said you wanted to tell them once it was all over. I wanted to meet them, and I knew they'd want to see where you were living and that you're okay."

Her dad was smiling at her and her mom was wringing her hands together. Maria's eyes filled with tears as she made her way to them.

"Maria." They wrapped her up in a hug, both wrapping their arms around her at once.

She lost herself in their familiar embrace. It'd been way too long since she'd seen them.

Her dad stood back and smiled at Zack. "Thank you for inviting us."

Zack shook his hand and bent down to kiss her mom's cheeks. "Thank you for coming."

"How did you even get here?" asked Maria.

Her mom smiled at Marianne. "I have an old friend who wanted to help out."

Her dad nodded and looked at Clay. "And we know a very generous man who didn't mind giving us a ride in his plane."

Clay smiled around at them. "I'm just happy to be able to play a small part in—" She felt Zack tense behind her as Clay obviously pulled himself up before he continued. "In all this."

Marianne smiled at her and took Clay's hand. "We'll talk to you later," she said before leading Clay away.

"Thank you for coming," Zack said again to her parents. He was nervous, she could tell. But her parents didn't seem too upset. In fact, they were both beaming and happy.

Her dad grasped Zack's shoulder and walked him away, leaving Maria alone with her mom. "I'm sorry I didn't tell you, Mom."

Her mom smiled and wrapped an arm around her waist. "That's okay, Maria. We understand. Zack explained. You know your father and I only want to see you happy. Zack's a good man. Marianne told us all about him, but even if she hadn't, you can just tell he's a good man. He's from a good family."

"I believe he is, but I haven't met …" She gave her mom a puzzled look. "How do you know?"

She could only describe the way her mom smiled as mysterious. She pointed to the man sitting with Eddie and April. "We've met his father."

"When? Just now? How long … when did you arrive?"

Her mom gave her that same smile. "Yesterday afternoon. You know how your Zack went out with Luke last night?"

Maria nodded.

"Well, he didn't just see Luke."

She had to laugh. "Well, isn't he the little schemer." A wave
of warmth spread through her chest. She felt like the luckiest
girl on earth just to be with him. To know that he'd gone to all
this trouble just to give her a housewarming party like this—
that he'd known how concerned she'd been about telling her
parents, and that he'd managed to get them here and smooth
things over with them before she even saw them.

"He's a good man, Maria."

"And you don't mind that we're living here—together—in
sin?"

Her mom pursed her lips. "You know I can never tell you
that I approve of that."

Maria should have known better than to ask. She couldn't
ask her mom to change her beliefs. She'd just have to be
grateful that she wasn't trying to impose them too strongly.

"I don't want to disappoint you, *Mamá.*"

Her mom gave her that weird smile again. "You haven't.
You make me very proud."

~ ~ ~

Maria's dad walked Zack over to his own dad who got to his
feet and smiled at them. For a moment, the three of them
stood there smiling at each other.

Zack's dad broke the silence first. "I haven't met your
daughter yet, Alberto. But I'm already proud of her."

"As am I. You won't be disappointed when you get to know
her."

"I feel like I already do. My son has loved her for a long
time."

Alberto smiled at Zack. "I wish I'd known from the beginning. I wouldn't have worried about her so much if I had."

Zack nodded. "I couldn't tell her how I felt. But now I want the whole world to know. I'm sorry I couldn't come to you earlier, to tell you and to ask you."

Alberto smiled. "The past is in the past. Now there's no more hiding. I know, her mom knows, and you know that you have our blessing—and our approval. So, how much longer are you going to wait?"

Zack grinned at him. "Not another minute."

He made his way over to Laura who was standing just outside the kitchen door with Smoke.

"Are you ready?" she asked.

Zack had to swallow around the lump that had formed in his throat.

She handed him the box, and he tried to clear his throat before he spoke.

Smoke grinned at him. "Don't bother trying to pull yourself together. You're going to turn into a ball of mush. It happens to the best of us. No one's judging. We know."

Luke stood beside him in the doorway and nodded. "It's true. Now go do it."

He looked around for Maria. She was standing talking to her mom and Marianne. He tapped his dad and Alberto on the shoulder as he passed them. "Come on. This is it."

Maria was laughing with her mom as Marianne told them how nervous she'd been the first time Clay had come to her house. She stopped when she saw Zack approaching them with his dad and hers following on his heels. Her heart started to race. She could only hope that they hadn't gotten into a disagreement about something.

The way Zack smiled at her told her there was nothing to worry about.

When he reached her, he nodded at Marianne and her mom. To her surprise, her mom reached up to kiss his cheeks before she and Marianne moved away.

When they'd gone, Zack took hold of her hand and gave her that weird look. It set her heart racing. She still hadn't figured out what it meant when he looked at her that way.

"Is something wrong?"

"No! Hell, no! Nothing's wrong, things couldn't be more right. Well, except for one thing."

He was making her nervous. He looked around at everyone, and she followed his gaze. Everyone had stopped talking and they were all watching them. She looked back at Zack; her heart was racing out of control. She didn't get what was going on.

He squeezed her hands and then got down on one knee and she finally understood. One hand came up to cover her mouth, but he kept a tight hold of the other one and smiled up at her.

She smiled back. She couldn't believe it, and yet it felt so perfectly right.

"Maria." His voice sounded gruff and scratchy. He tried again. "Maria. You know I love you. I've already told you you're stuck with me."

She nodded and the tears started to roll down her cheeks.

"I promised you forever, and I meant it. We haven't had the easiest start, but that's only proved how good we are together, how strong we are, and how much I love you. I'm going to love you till the day I die, and I'm going to do my best to make you happy every single day. Please tell me you want it, too. Say you'll be my wife? Will you marry me?"

"Yes!" She nodded like a crazy person. "Yes. Of course, I'll marry you."

He slid the ring onto her finger and got to his feet. His arms closed around her and she reached hers up around his neck to pull him down into a kiss. It didn't matter who was watching: her parents, his, all their friends—they all disappeared as she and Zack got lost in that kiss.

When they finally came up for air, he landed a peck on her forehead. "Do you like it?"

She didn't know what he meant until he tugged on her finger, and she looked down. "Holy shit!" She pressed her lips tight shut and looked around, hoping no one had heard. Of course, they had and were all laughing.

She looked up into his eyes. "It's gorgeous, Zack! It's …" She'd worked in a jewelry store her entire adult life. She knew her diamonds, and the one sitting on her finger was no less than three carats. "I don't need all that."

He cupped his hands around the sides of her neck and looked down into her eyes. "Maybe not. But you deserve it."

"It's true." His dad had come to congratulate them, as had her parents. "I don't know you yet, Maria, but I already know that I'm proud to call you family." He leaned in to kiss her cheek and she took an instant liking to him.

"And I know I'm proud to call you family, too." She smiled. "I mean, look at the son you raised."

She'd hoped to make him happy, but instead his smile faded. "I'm not proud of the way I've affected his life."

Zack put his arm around his dad's shoulders. "I've told you and told you. None of it was your fault."

Maria hugged him. "He's right, you know. You aren't responsible for what Morales did. But you are responsible for having raised a wonderful son, and I'll be forever grateful to you."

Zack grinned. "I told you. She's a real positive peanut. She'll find the bright side in anything."

His dad laughed as she slapped Zack's arm. "I am not a peanut."

Her parents hugged them both.

"We're so happy for you," said her mom.

Maria laughed as it dawned on her. "And this is why you didn't mind us living together. You knew, didn't you?"

They nodded. "Zack asked us, and we gave him our blessing."

She smiled up at him. "You have been a busy boy this week, haven't you?"

He laughed. "It was tough to pull it all off with you trying to play nursemaid the whole time—not that I'm complaining about that," he added hastily.

She slid her arm around his waist and leaned against him. "I should know by now just how good you are at hiding things."

He hugged her into his side. "Not anymore. I'm done hiding. I lost too many years hiding from Morales. I hid my heart from you for longer than I could bear. I should have waited until my past was all dealt with, but I couldn't do it."

She looked up into his eyes and smiled. "That's because between you and me, there's just too much love to hide.";

;

A Note from SJ

I hope you enjoyed Maria and Zack's story. Please let your friends know about the books if you feel they would enjoy them as well. It would be wonderful if you would leave me a review, I'd very much appreciate it.

There are so many more stories still to tell. I can tell you that the Nashville folks finally got tired of waiting. They've pushed Autumn and Matt to the forefront, and no matter how much Autumn tried to resist it, their book will be next. There is also a bunch of cowboys growing very impatient in Montana. And there's another more mature couple who are eager to add to the Silver series soon. That's without even thinking about Grady, who would like the Hamiltons series to be at least five books long. And Spider, from the Davenports series—he's no millionaire but he so deserves his own book and will get one. If you know me at all, you'll know that planning and organization are not my strong suits. However, I'm working on it! I'll let you know when I figure it out.

In the meantime, check out the "Also By" page to see if any of my other series appeal to you – I have a couple of freebie series starters, too, so you can take them for a test drive.

There are a few options to keep up with me and my imaginary friends:

The best way is to Sign up for my Newsletter at my website www.SJMcCoy.com. Don't worry I won't bombard you! I'll let you know about upcoming releases, share a sneak peek or two and keep you in the loop for a couple of fun giveaways I have coming up :0)

You can join my readers group to chat about the books or like my Facebook Page

I occasionally attempt to say something in 140 characters or less(!) on Twitter

And I'm in the process of building a shiny new website at www.SJMcCoy.com

I love to hear from readers, so feel free to email me at SJ@SJMcCoy.com if you'd like. I'm better at that! :0)

I hope our paths will cross again soon. Until then, take care, and thanks for your support—you are the reason I write!

Love

SJ

PS Project Semicolon

You may have noticed that the final sentence of the story closed with a semi-colon. It isn't a typo. <u>Project Semi Colon</u> is a non-profit movement dedicated to presenting hope and love to those who are struggling with depression, suicide, addiction and self-injury. Project Semicolon exists to encourage, love and inspire. It's a movement I support with all my heart.

"A semicolon represents a sentence the author could have ended, but chose not to. The sentence is your life and the author is you." - Project Semicolon

This author started writing after her son was killed in a car crash. At the time I wanted my own story to be over, instead I chose to honour a promise to my son to write my 'silly stories' someday. I chose to escape into my fictional world. I know for many who struggle with depression, suicide can appear to be the only escape. The semicolon has become a symbol of support, and hopefully a reminder – Your story isn't over yet

Also by SJ McCoy

Summer Lake Seasons
Angel and Luke in Take These Broken Wings
Zack and Maria in Too Much Love to Hide

Summer Lake Silver
Clay and Marianne in Like Some Old Country Song

Summer Lake Series
Love Like You've Never Been Hurt (FREE in ebook form)
Work Like You Don't Need the Money
Dance Like Nobody's Watching
Fly Like You've Never Been Grounded
Laugh Like You've Never Cried
Sing Like Nobody's Listening
Smile Like You Mean It
The Wedding Dance
Chasing Tomorrow
Dream Like Nothing's Impossible
Ride Like You've Never Fallen
Live Like There's No Tomorrow
The Wedding Flight

Remington Ranch Series
Mason (FREE in ebook form) and also available as Audio
Shane
Carter
Beau
Four Weddings and a Vendetta

A Chance and a Hope

Chance is a guy with a whole lot of story to tell. He's part of the fabric of both Summer Lake and Remington Ranch. He needed three whole books to tell his own story.

Chance Encounter
Finding Hope
Give Hope a Chance

The Davenports

Oscar
TJ
Reid

The Hamiltons

Cameron and Piper in Red wine and Roses
Chelsea and Grant in Champagne and Daisies
Mary Ellen and Antonio in Marsala and Magnolias
Marcos and Molly in Prosecco and Peonies
Coming Next
Grady

Love In Nashville

Matt and Autumn in Bring on the Night

About the Author

I'm SJ, a coffee addict, lover of chocolate and drinker of good red wines. I'm a lost soul and a hopeless romantic. Reading and writing are necessary parts of who I am. Though perhaps not as necessary as coffee! I can drink coffee without writing, but I can't write without coffee.

I grew up loving romance novels, my first boyfriends were book boyfriends, but life intervened, as it tends to do, and I wandered down the paths of non-fiction for many years. My life changed completely a few years ago and I returned to Romance to find my escape.

I write 'Sweet n Steamy' stories because to me there is enough angst and darkness in real life. My favorite romances are happy escapes with a focus on fun, friendships and happily-ever-afters, just like the ones I write.

These days I live in beautiful Montana, the last best place. If I'm not reading or writing, you'll find me just down the road in the park - Yellowstone. I have deer, eagles and the occasional bear for company, and I like it that way :0)

Made in the
USA
Middletown, DE